Stinging Fly Patrons

Many thanks to: Maria Behan, Niamh Black, John Boyne, Celine Broughal, Trish Byrne, Bruce Carolan, Edmond Condon, Evelyn Conlon, Edel Fairclough, Michael J. Farrell, Ciara Ferguson, Kathy Gilfillan, Michael Gillen, Brendan Hackett, James Hanley, Dennis Houlihan, Nuala Jackson, Claire Keegan, Jerry Kelleher, Conor Kennedy, Gráinne Killeen, Joe Lawlor, Irene Rose Ledger, Wendy Lynch, Róisín McDermott, Petra McDonough, Lynn Mc Grane, Finbar McLoughlin, Maggie McLoughlin, Ama, Grace & Fraoch Mac Sweeney, Mary Mac Sweeney, Paddy & Moira Mac Sweeney, Anil Malhotra, Dáirine Ní Mheadhra, Nessa O'Mahony, Lucy Perrem, Maria Pierce, Peter J. Pitkin, Fiona Ruff, Ann Seery, Eileen Sheridan, Alfie & Savannah Stephenson, Mike Timms, Olive Towey, Simon Trewin, Ruth Webster, Gráinne Wilson, The Irish Centre for Poetry Studies at Mater Dei Institute, Lilliput Press, Munster Literature Centre, New Binary Press, Poetry Ireland, Tramp Press and Trashface Books.

We'd also like to thank those individuals who have expressed the preference to remain anonymous.

By making an annual contribution of 75 euro, patrons provide us with vital support and encouragement.

Become a patron online at
www.stingingfly.org
or send a cheque or postal order to:

The Stinging Fly, PO Box 6016, Dublin 1.

issue 29 / volume two
Winter 2014-15

COVER DESIGN

Fergal Condon

SINCE LAST ISSUE: In July, Colin Barrett won the Frank O'Connor International Short Story Award for his brilliant collection *Young Skins*, which we published in 2013. Then, last month, he went and won the Rooney Prize for Irish Literature. If you see him, shake his hand.

NEXT ISSUE: Our next issue will appear in February 2014. Submissions and pitches for the Summer 2015 London Issue are being accepted until October 31, 2014. Full guidelines can be found on our website: www.stingingfly.org

'… God has specially appointed me to this city, so as though it were a large thoroughbred horse which because of its great size is inclined to be lazy and needs the stimulation of some stinging fly…'

—Plato, *The Last Days of Socrates*

The Stinging Fly
new writers, new writing

Editor
Thomas Morris

Poetry Editor
Eabhan Ní Shúileabháin

Eagarthóir filíochta Gaeilge
Aifric Mac Aodha

Editorial Assistant
Lily Ní Dhomhnaill

Publisher
Declan Meade

Design & Layout
Fergal Condon

Contributing Editors
Emily Firetog, Dave Lordan & Sean O'Reilly

Rachel McNicholl's translation of Frank Schulz's story was supported by the Goethe Institut Irland. The story was originally published as 'Männertreu' in *Mehr Liebe: Heikle Geschichten* by Galiani, Berlin.

© 2010, Kiepenheuer & Witsch GmbH & Co. KG, Cologne/Germany.

Printed by Naas Printing Ltd.

ISBN 978-1-906539-43-6 ISSN 1393-5690

Published three times a year (February, June and October).

The Stinging Fly gratefully acknowledges the support of The Arts Council/ An Chomhairle Ealaíon and Dublin City Council.

PO Box 6016, Dublin 1
stingingfly@gmail.com

Keep in touch: sign up to our e-mail newsletter, become a fan on Facebook, or follow us on Twitter for regular updates about all our publications, events and activities.

www.stingingfly.org | www.facebook.com/StingingFly | @stingingfly

Editorial

Open an anthology of new writing, turn to the introduction, and you'll likely encounter a closing sentence along the lines of: '... *but if these works are anything to go by, the future of literature is in safe hands!*' Prior to this sentence, the editor will probably have expounded on the notion that literature is close to death, or—more painfully (for the writers, at least)—being perpetually ignored. And so, 'the safe hands' sentence is meant to reassure us. We can rest easy, it says, because things will be okay.

But safe hands are the last things that art needs.

Indeed, the most thrilling moments in writing are when the author is veritably un-safe, and takes a leap—in plot, character, logic, language or whatever—and reveals *something* (perhaps, even, our own selves).

Of course, the editors probably don't mean 'safe writing' when they say 'safe hands'—but the statement still possesses, I feel, an implicit suggestion that literature is a kind of Olympic torch, and that by being included in the said anthology / collection, the authors are lining up to carry the Good Light of Art into the dark depths of an uncaring world. These authors, the editors seem to say, are the chosen ones now. Bow down and watch their safe hands at work.

My god, is there anything more annoying for the unpublished writer to hear? That whiff of clique, the suggestion of a group hand-holding party that they're not invited to?

The hands in this Issue 29 are not safe. They are strange, sly, cruel, panicked, doleful, jealous, ecstatic, earnest, aggressive, selfish and incredibly dextrous. They tremble with story. And by right, they have no business being beside other limbs, lined up neatly in a magazine. If they had it their way, you wouldn't be touching—or even looking at—someone else's hands.

I had worried that the writings here were all a little *too* idiosyncratic, a little too odd. But then, the best works of literature have always been ones that are strange in their own unique ways. They make their own rules. And that taste of the illicit—that wholly audacious element—is what gives them their *frisson*.

(I should add that 'illicit' and 'audacious' aren't my bywords for a host of stories about people having sex in car parks. One of the most devastating sentences I've ever encountered appears in the film *Tokyo Story*. At a funeral, one character quietly remarks to another, 'Isn't life disappointing?' At first glance, it might seem like an unremarkable statement. We are accustomed to sentiments like, 'Wasn't the match disappointing?' or 'I was disappointed that we had to shoot the dog'—but to say, so baldly, so succinctly, that life—*our entire human existence*—is 'disappointing'. Well, it takes a moment to register... but then...)

Done with skill, the smallest things—a moment of silence, a comma, or even a paragraph break—can cause the greatest unease.

*

As *The Stinging Fly* achieves more prominence, it inevitably runs the risk of becoming The Establishment—the 'safe hands' for emerging 'safe-hands writing'. Our challenge, as I see it, is to continue to publish the best new writing, but to do so—in the way of great art itself—boldly and without apologies. To hell with playing safe.

—Thomas Morris, October 2014

Essay | Raising the Devil: The unspeakable fictions of Liam O'Flaherty

Dave Lordan

Thank you so much for your letter and cheque. I would be dead were it not for you
and of course Fr John O Reilly would say you were aiding and abetting the devil.
Well, I hope to raise the devil with the world yet anyway.

—A letter from Liam O'Flaherty to Edward Garnett, June 1923

Imagine a France where the name Celine hardly ever popped up in literary conversations; or a Norway where Hamsun was not taught on university literature courses; or an Italy where *The Leopard* had been out of print for forty years and could only be found by chancing across it in a second-hand book store or by painstakingly trawling through the online catalogues of rare book dealers; or a Russia where no book-length critical study of Dostoevsky has been published since 1976. Imagine, indeed, any country where the writer who left behind the most comprehensive and provocative literary record of the most momentous events in its modern history had been all but forgotten in its wider culture. You will have guessed that such a country does exist, and it is now called the Republic of Ireland, though it is far from the Republic of Ireland that insurrectionists took up arms for in 1916. Insurrectionist Liam O'Flaherty is Irish modernism's forgotten great writer, and that forgetting has not been a natural process, but is intimately connected with the operational priorities of the Irish culture industry.

The Tom and Liam O'Flaherty Society have recently initiated the vital process of commemorating O'Flaherty through events and re-publications. Apart from this small column of dedicatees however, O'Flaherty and his legacy are blanketed in silence. The answer to the riddle of his exclusion from our cultural narrative is obvious. It's because of his uncompromisingly radical politics, and, more broadly, the nihilistic, anti-romantic, Nietzschean philosophical outlook which animates his most important works. This makes him generally inappropriate for commemorative honour by the state, or by any in the decisive upper echelons of arts admin who depend on state patronage, and whom the state in return depends on to farm our literary heritage for ceremonious prestige.

'Let us not be ashamed that gunshots are heard in our streets. Let us rather be glad. For force is, after all, the opposite of sluggishness. It is an intensity of movement, of motion. And motion is the opposite of death,' writes O'Flaherty in a letter to the *Irish Statesman* in 1924, arguing that great cultural progress only occurs in periods of, and because of, warfare. Warfare is broadly defined in O'Flaherty's imagination and depicted in his fiction as the struggle between humankind and nature, as well as the endless human wars between nations, classes, families, couples, and within the fragmented individual mind. As in Shakespeare and Homer, struggle between warring opposites is the constant core and dynamo of O'Flaherty's narratives. Altogether, O'Flaherty's fiction, from *Famine* to *The Assassin*, forms the Epic, or the History Play, of Ireland from the 1840s to the 1920s. This is the foundational period when the independent Irish state, now embarking on a ten-year celebratory misremembering of itself, was born in a hail of bombs and bullets, some of them aimed by, and at, Liam O'Flaherty.

His *Irish Statesman* letter proposes the same dialectic of history later put forward in a more toastmasterly fashion by Walter Benjamin, that *every document of civilisation is at the same time a document of barbarism*. Whereas Benjamin's instinct is to lament this basic truth of social evolution, O'Flaherty proclaims it without any kind of tears or shame. For him, in art and in life, conflict between warring parties is the generator powering an inevitable process of perpetual mutation. In his fiction O'Flaherty strove to root this philosophy of history (and cosmos) in depictions of the lived historical experience of his period; to, as Marx put it, *rise from the abstract to the concrete*. In his 1932 masterpiece *Skerrett*, which pivots on the struggle between a Machiavellian priest and an idealistic national school teacher for the control over the bodies and souls of the peasantry of the Island of Nara, O'Flaherty writes that 'it must be remembered that this was the period when the whole of Ireland began to emerge from feudalism, as the result of the guerrilla war waged by the peasants against the landowners. Even in Nara […] the will towards civilisation had been stirred into life.' The idea that Irish modernity emerged from the partisan struggle of our very poorest and most desperate and above all anonymous past citizens, rather than from the actions of a line of Great and Holy Men stretching from O'Connell to Lemass wouldn't suit either mass-market biographers or Hollywood. It is far too unsettling a proposal to be included in the state-managed 'debates' on Irish history which will form a central ritual and TV-spectacular element of the ongoing centennials.

In O'Flaherty's furiously-paced fictions of clash and mutability, nothing is ever allowed to settle or fix form for too long; there is no peace, no rest, no lengthy contemplative passages, no ikon-making. No character is ever allowed to triumph for long, no relationship is stable, no institution is not designed to implode in the end. Always in the darkly roaring interstices of his sentences one hears the coast-destroying winds and the man-devouring seas of the western seaboard as they continue their ceaseless reshaping of everything, including themselves. O'Flaherty mostly succeeds in avoiding pietistic, mystical or comical images of the picturesquely downtrodden Irish; these three stratagems being, then as now, the dominant representational modes of our literature. Rather, he aims, in his fictional and philosophical obsession with struggle, violence, and transformation, to flow-map the unstoppable metamorphosing torrent of history itself.

Unsurprisingly then, O'Flaherty is highly unusual among Dead Irish Giants in that he has little by way of homely, monetisable snippets to offer Bord Fáilte and beermat purveyors. He is, in fact, the anti-Bord Fáilte. His parodic masterpiece *A Tourists Guide to Ireland*, the best English-language satire written in Ireland since Swift's *A Tale of a Tub*, is scathingly accurate about our state in its days of formation. That it is now practically an unknown text is hardly a coincidence. O'Flaherty despised the real, benighted Ireland with the same passion as others worshipped the largely invented Ireland of the Celtic Twilight. Where Synge saw 'wild paradise', O'Flaherty gives us the truer Connaught of Oliver Cromwell, a wind-blasted hell where dignified life was impossible. O'Flaherty's peasants have no more to do with the Fianna than absentee landlords had to do with famine relief. They are starving, conniving, avaricious, ignorant, wife-bashing drunks who live with pigs and can think of no reason why they shouldn't. His post-1923 revolutionaries are grotesque factionalists, using idealism to mask vengeful bloodlust. His primary school teachers are brutal sadists who detest children and drive them to suicide. His politicians and businessmen are gombeens one and all. His priests are politicians and businessmen. His artists and writers are mystic quacks and second-hand priests. His gardaí are, well, the luckiest of pigs, having migrated from the blow-away mud huts to the wind-impregnable fortress of the barracks. O'Flaherty understood the Ireland of the revolutionary and post-revolutionary period better—and depicted it with a more ruthless fidelity—than any other writer ever has.

Perhaps O'Flaherty's most significant departure from our three major literary traditions (the Latin and Gaelic monastic, the Gaelic bardic, and the post-conquest Anglo Irish) is his conception of nature, specifically the unconsoling nature of rural and Atlantic Ireland. O'Flaherty's Irish nature is godless and hostile, a mocking serial destroyer of all human ambition and achievement. When David Skerrett stands abandoned and derided by the people of Nara, whom he has fought so long and so bitterly to civilise, O'Flaherty, in a typical mock-Wordsworthian move, has him seek escape from and consolation for human disappointment in the raw sublimity of our Atlantic Coast:

> Suddenly, he thought that the earth was a living being, making fun of his defeat. All was so silent and mysterious and unapproachable. He thought how puny and weak was man, wandering haphazard on this cruel earth, pressing its face with his feet, burrowing in its bosom and then passing to his death, when the vain quests of his life have dissolved in horrid annihilation. And it was made manifest to him as he watched the glistening crust of sun-baked rock, beneath its dome of sky, that there was no God to reward the just or to punish the wicked, nothing beyond this unconquerable earth but the phantasies born of man's fear and man's vanity. And he began to laugh softly to himself.

This is, of course, Schopenhauer in Inishmore, with the laughter of derangement added. In the Irish West, we leap laughingly into our sacrilegiously bottomless wells.

O'Flaherty is by far the most off-message, the most debunking and desacrilising of the great Irish writers; no one clinging to power in art or in politics, or in art-politics, wants to hear from the likes of him, or for the likes of him to be heard. To me, there's a clear continuity between the censors of the 1920s and the most bureaucratized and market-oriented sections of today's Irish culture industry. O'Flaherty is administratively forgotten today by the direct descendants of those who banned him in the 1920s, working out of the same offices. The modus operandi may have evolved, but the effect is the same—the awkward are silenced. O'Flaherty's status as our great unknown author is, on the one hand, a huge tribute to his continuing ability to disturb those whom culturally-significant artists are born to disturb, and on the other hand testimony in the cultural sphere to the accuracy of Brendan Behan's contention that in 1923 'nothing changed but the badge on the warder's cap'.

The Morning After

I want to stop hearing
the footsteps of the rejected
shuffle around empty apartments
in their dressing gowns,
clutching their phones for fear
they'll miss *that* call,
the 'I miss you too' call.

I want to stop hearing the sound of
late night restaurant workers clocking out,
carrying half-loaves under their arms.
I do not want them to miss the last tube tonight.
I don't want to hear the sound of
people on night buses,
or to think of keys turning in doors
where all the milk's gone
and there's no sugar for the tea.

I want people to get home safe tonight,
to catch the news at six,
to place their heartbreaks and payslips
in the drawer beneath the cutlery,
the one reserved for old stubs of birthday candles,
batteries and Blu-Tack.

I want to reverse the shuffle
of the night-gowned dejected
and mix it with some smokey blues.
I want them to wash their hair, go out,
drink something short and neat,
cry while singing Macy Gray
but still get picked up at the end of the night.

I want to know that everybody has to do this same shuffle—
to come to on a stranger's couch,
pick your way over the bodies,
drink what's left of the mixers,
walk out the door
and start again.

Esther Waters

Lay Down The Dark Layers
Deborah Rose Reeves

Claret

The piece is perhaps a landscape, certainly not a portrait or that of a figure, but briefly she imagines she has happened across a corpse in the bathtub, not a painting. Specks of crimson and claret spatter the white enamel, in which an easel looms, its subject flayed and seeping russet, red ochre, raw umber, burnt umber.

She runs the tap until it steams then rubs between her legs with a rough cloth. There is no soap, only a clutter of brushes in a can of turpentine. She cleans her teeth with her finger and stares into the mirror. Her mouth is still plum from the wine they drank. I am a landscape too, she thinks, scratching at the crests and valley of her top lip.

Insects And Grass

Scrabbling for her shoes in the gloom, she cast short glances at the man asleep in the bed. She'd known him to see. The rest of the details were dim—only his hand on her thigh and the winking lights of College Green as the taxi rounded onto Pearse Street and tore through the night towards the docklands.

She had not been this downriver since her father had brought her and her brother to see the tall ships passing through. She couldn't believe that people lived here now, was bewitched by the reflection of the water on so many new windows and, once inside the apartment, she held her head so she could see the silvery stillness the entire time she was there until she was walking out the door again.

Outside she began to run, looking this way and that for a roaming taxi to take her back into the city or home. There was no urgency, she had no place to be, but she liked the image and how she believed she must look to anyone who might see her—glassy-eyed, sparkle-dressed, a girl running wild in the predawn.

Crossing onto Lower Mount Street she was stilled mid-flight by the copper fur of a fox beneath a streetlight, its green eyes regarding her from amidst a litter of peelings and scraps. She had heard of urban foxes, of the den by the Dáil, how they scavenged for whatever they could get and would eat insects and grass if nothing else were available. But she had never seen one in real life.

What Happened To You Anyway?

In the morning she looked into the mirror and the face of girl stared back and winced when she saw what she had not felt. Her fingertips rose to her cheekbone, beguiled. Her eye was a perfect plum with streaks of black mascara and specks of fine glitter that she washed away. Then, pressing nearer to the glass and considering it more closely, she took in the pretty print of fuchsia, mustard, grass, and periwinkle. Last night's clothes lay scattered all around.

In the kitchen, her flatmate regarded her from behind a cigarette and a French Press.

I see you got home okay then, she said.

I couldn't find you. When I got back from the toilets you weren't on the dance floor.

I must've been off looking for you, she said, stubbing out the half-smoked butt.

That's so weird. I looked all around. I'd got a drink for you.

So you went to the bar or you went to the dance floor?

Jesus, I don't know. God.

They sat in silence with coffee and an ashtray between them, picking at their little bowls of plain yoghurt and fruit.

What happened to you anyway? asked her flatmate, finally.

Oh this? she said. I'm not really sure.

At work the women in the break room gathered around her. Let's just say there was a headboard involved, she said, and they all whispered Jesus through their teeth.

Does he have a brother? said Margaret who was like a mother to them. Or a father? And they cried laughing then went back to their desks and thought the day would never come to an end.

Don't tell mam, she said to her sister on the phone.

I can't believe he gave you a black eye, said her sister. Who is this person?

That's the thing, she said, touching her fingers to her face again. She was tired and the night before seemed long ago. It's everything but black. It's all these other colours.

Portrait

Barmen called him by his name and knew what he wanted to drink. He paid for his first drink only but was never without a glass before him. He was not ashamed for a woman to ask what he was having and he stood unconcerned in the face of a round. It was the rare man who interrupted when he was speaking. Often a girl would grab her coat and leave in a hurry, while others would linger until just after he'd left, pretending not to notice him from evening until closing. He was despised by many but repudiated by no one.

There is a man like this in every pub and corner of the country.

And The Thing Is

She'd say to people, I hadn't even thought about him that much.

Though she wasn't in the habit of them, she was very understanding about one-night stands: things happened, they didn't mean anything. Sometime later, though, she had popped into Hogans after work and caught his eye at the other end of the bar. Dublin is a small town—she offered what she thought was a knowing but mollifying smile and expected that to be the end of it, in that she expected him to offer her something similar in return. Rather, he looked at her as though to say, The fuck you lookin' at me for?

And the question opened what had been closed, revealing a space that a part of her rushed to inhabit. And this left its own space and that, too, generated a void. And this accounted for the shame and longing that emptied and filled her as she waited to pay for her drink, and the thirst with which she drank it, and the apparent nonchalance with which she ordered another.

And later, during a chance meeting on the stairs in which words were exchanged, she was so relieved by what she now assumed had been her own misunderstanding that she did not object to him pulling her into the ladies' bathroom and pressing her up against the wall.

I'm On My Way

Pale blossoms followed the bright berries of winter and fell away, too soon. The shimmering mirage of summer: diaphanous rain. The days and months moved on and she imagined she moved in pace with them. But here we see her in September, a barman is calling last orders please and she is saying goodnight to friends and waiting for a message that asks is she around. She is. She is always around, or can be. She is in the same place. The place that answers I'm on my way. It is the same night as the first night, the same night as the last. A hundred and one one-nights. The light and the breeze and the blossoms bend around her as they press on.

Their Situation

She enjoyed the sensation of stepping into a museum or gallery—parquet floors announcing her arrival and passage from room to room where high ceilings amplified all things, from the tickle in her throat to the timid stirrings of her soul. It was a small joy, available to anyone, and costing nothing, which was perhaps why they were so often very empty and she herself had only thought to pay a visit once she started sleeping with the painter on a regular basis.

Sleeping with an artist was different than she thought. She had pictured so many sketches of herself, scattered in a light-filled place: reading a book, stepping into a bathtub, removing an earring, seated, standing. She imagined what it would be like to pose for him, saw him lean in to fix a falling hair, moving her this way and that, though she supposed he did in his own way.

Still, she hoped they might sometimes do other things together too, but she didn't know how to invite him to join her without giving the wrong impression. She wanted it to be clear that she understood their situation. So she would only sometimes mention that she was thinking of going to such and such exhibition, and she would never say that she had been—unless to say she had been there with a friend—so that he wouldn't think of her as someone who was often alone.

Sometimes she thought of herself alone in those long, tall rooms, her face raised to the rows of gilded frames, and it was beautiful. She liked this unexpected life. Her eye fell upon new shelves in bookshops and she sought out others in the library. She began to acquire a new vocabulary and way of seeing things; yet this, too, presented a problem. Having finally found something she might say to him, she found she could not say it. A sudden allusion to Caravaggio might strike him as peculiar. *Pentimenti* is an awkward word to work into a sentence when somebody has an idea of who you are already.

3AM

Whatever happened to your painting? she asked into the dark.

Why? he said, after a few seconds.

I was just thinking about it, she said.

It's late, he said.

A few minutes later he sighed, turned on the lamp and left the room. When he came back with the canvas under his arm she sat up and clapped and he shook his head. He climbed back into bed and set it between them. It had not changed much since the first time she had seen it. Her fingers hovered over it.

Don't touch, he said.

I know, she said, though she did want to place her hands on it and feel the thin scratches and depressions that textured the surface. Several times, she could see, he had painted a layer, then waited for it to dry before taking to it with something rough. In a few trace places he had scratched through the deep browns and iron reds to reveal the canvas beneath. Dark mottling suggested rocks in a fallow field but it was not discernibly of anything.

She looked at him and smiled through sudden tears.

Is it finished? she said.

No, he said. He picked up the painting and set it on the floor. First you lay down the dark layers and then you add light. It can take a while. He switched off the lamp and turned away.

Her eyes adjusted again to the gloom.

Hey, she said.

What? he said.

Thank you.

Her Sister Said

What happened to his teeth?

And she said, What do you mean?

He's missing two of his teeth, she said. She tongued her top and bottom teeth, counting and thinking. It's like this one, and this one, she said, placing the curled tip of her tongue on one tooth and another.

I don't know, she said. I never noticed it.

She said she would look the next time she saw him but the next time she saw him she forgot to look.

Her Old, Dear Friend

Her old, dear friend set his glass on the table and kicked at the legs of the stool she was sitting on across from him.

What the fuck? she laughed, but his eyes did not return her smile.

You're always looking over my shoulder, he said.

What?

When we're out. When I'm talking. You're always looking just past me.

No I'm not, she said. Am I?

He's not even here, said her friend and picked up his drink and looked away.

They sat like this for what seemed a long time, looking around the room and into their drinks. Finally, she kicked at the legs of his stool and made a sad face to see if he would smile.

Patronage

For a third week the rain was preventing him from working. For money he paint-ed houses and nobody had their doors or windows done in this weather.

Fuckin' rain, he said. What could he do?

She asked him about the insides or other odd jobs, bar work maybe.

Sure nobody's the money to be painting their kitchens every five minutes any-more, he said, taking a long drag from a joint and passing it to her. They're stuck with their fuckin' persimmon now aren't they?

She supposed so.

C'mere to me, he said.

In the morning, before she left for work herself, she set two tens between the teabags and the sugar. She thought to leave more but this way he might think it was his own that he'd forgotten. Either way, he never mentioned anything about it.

A couple of weeks later he was shy of his rent.

It's not like he asked me for it, she thought, licking the envelope. He was just talking and I was just there.

Thank you thank you thank you, he said.

She spoke to her father whose mother's house was sitting idle. It might sell quicker if they had a bit of work done—she had a friend who could start right away.

She thought of him in his paint-spattered overalls in her nana's old kitchen, lis-tening to the small, portable radio, milky tea pouring from the teapot, so familiar.

Her sister sent her a message when she was at work. Dad was going mad. Globs of paint and plaster were ground into the floor. The sink was clogged with the stuff. There were dirty dishes on the counter, brushes and rollers stuck to trays of dried paint. He's not going to pay for this crap, said her sister.

I've already paid him, she wrote back. I'm on my way.

She called him from the taxi and tried to explain things from her father's point of view. How it was his mother's house, and what that meant to him, so it was hard to see the place just left that way. He said he was sorry, he'd planned to go back and clean it up but had got a call about another job and couldn't turn it down.

You know what it's been like, he said. What could he have done?

Her father and sister had cleaned the house and gone by the time she got there. She let herself in and stood in the small kitchen, transformed completely from her memory of it. The windows were bare of their faded net curtains. The grimy wallpaper had been stripped spare. He'd filled in the parts in the walls that had crumbled, painted them a delicate colour she would never have thought of. It was brighter and more open, as she'd hoped. It was good work.

On George's Street, An Encounter

She wandered into Dunnes and placed in the basket the makings of a meal: stewing beef, onions, carrots, russets, crusty bread and butter, wine. She tried to picture his kitchen, what might or might not be in it, but could only see her hand around a glass and the cold tap running in the middle of the night. She picked up a box of salt and considered it then replaced it on the shelf and walked away. She returned the wine and chose a different bottle then went back for the salt and noticed, on the way, a large pot on sale that got her thinking about utensils.

Standing in the checkout line, she composed a text but was called to pay before she could send it. Out on the street, she fumbled with her bags and phone when he appeared through the arch of the old shopping arcade and down towards her. A girl was walking with him. He touched her hip and steered her across the traffic to the other side of the road.

On the bus home, she looked down at her boots surrounded by paper bags filled with dresses and books and thank you cards and chocolate and something for her sister and all of the food for dinner and the big pot. And she felt a little sick from the fumes that come from the engine under the back seat but it is also warmest there and it was the beginning of winter.

Salt

An uncommon snow fell in November, softening steeples and iron railings, pillowing cobblestones and filling the cracks. Low clouds leached into rooftops, grey as the gulls that screeched from deep within them, displaced. They skittered on the air, wanting to settle but wary and resentful. The intricate expanse of streets and alleys was from afar a frozen lake, sighs and speculations echoing from its fissures.

People walked as though for the first time, hands stretched to steady them, ready to slide. Delighted at first, strangers smiled at each other in mutual commiseration. They laughed nervously or were quieted with wonder. The air was still and time appeared to stop but when life continued to make demands of them they became impatient and anxious for salt to arrive from Europe. They soon remembered the last year's unexpected cold snap. You'd think we'd have learned something, they said.

Desideratum

From desire, she murmured beneath her breath, her fingers following the small font across and down the soft, translucent page of an aged dictionary. From the Old French, *desirrer*: wish for, long for. From Latin, *desiderare*: long for, wish for, but also meaning demand, expect. Her eyes hovered over the words then continued down the page. Original sense was perhaps 'await what the stars will bring', from the phrase *de sidere*, 'from the stars', from *sidus*: star, constellation, heavenly body.

She set aside the heavy tome and scanned the article she'd been reading. She couldn't remember the sentence she'd paused upon, her reason for needing the dictionary in the first place. Distracted, she couldn't say how she'd got from there to here, not in so many words.

When she left the reading room, the clock in the front square struck the quarter hour. It was hardly past six but so dark as to seem deep night. It was strange to see that the day was not nearly done, that she had more time than she thought. She walked across the cobblestones, illuminated by the lamps in the arches of the college chapel and the campanile. She had not a single idea but that Dublin was loitering beyond the gates, waiting for her. Passing through the wooden entrance of the west door, she ignored the noticeboards overflowing with events fliers and invitations to various clubs and societies, and stepped out into the city and nowhere in particular.

The Coach & Ferry

There was nothing to be done. He would have to go to London. His flatmate had asked him to leave, a rancorous end to what had been a friendship. Sides had been taken in Grogan's and The Cobblestone: he owed everybody something. Twice he had moved back home but he couldn't be himself—they knew him too well. Where else can I go like?

You could stay with me but you know what my flatmate's like, she lied. She took him out to dinner and, later, lay in the crook of his arm, face pressed to his bony ribcage, rising and falling to the dull rhythms within, lulled to sleep by a long list of betrayals that thankfully didn't include her.

She did not know where he spent his last days and nights in Dublin. She had given him some little things for fun but they seemed foolish now when she thought of him on the coach and ferry—a string bag of chocolate coins in golden foil, and a small box of paints and a set of postcard-sized watercolour paper. She wrote her name and address on the first one and asked him to send her a little painting from somewhere better. When the postman came, and there was nothing for her, she was relieved to have been so soon forgotten.

I Am Here For You

She was the kind of girl that people unburdened themselves to while waiting for a bus. She found it difficult to extricate herself from the recounting of a grievance and often she settled into her seat, accepting that she was here till the end of the line with this one. She became frightened of being old. Women shared more resentments and men tended towards regret, though not remorse.

One night, a man stumbled up to her and asked if this was the stop to Rathmines; he thought he was staying at a Travelodge there. He didn't need to tell her he was on a stag weekend from England—a short-sleeved shirt on a winter night said it all and she hoped he would wander away again but he leaned against the wall beside her.

It was a rare night out for him, he said, and she smiled politely but looked away, waiting for the bit about the ball and chain. He was a night watchman at a hospital, he continued, and she commiserated about the strange hours, surrendering to being sucked into his life for a while. The hours were strange, he agreed, but he had chosen them. He was avoiding his family, he told her, a lovely wife and a daughter.

He loved them in his head, he said. He knew he did. But he felt nothing—nothing. Not even when the girl was a child. He knocked back a couple of cans every morning when he got home and slept into the evening. He didn't know what else to do. She didn't know what to tell him.

When the bus came he preferred to stand but he looked her way every few minutes until she nodded that this was his stop. He looked in through the window as the bus pulled away, as though to say now what? She pointed straight ahead, on your left and watched him follow her finger up the street of a place he didn't come from.

Midwinter

She wakes in the dark and lays there. A thin light flits and shrinks below her door as her flatmate makes her way to and from the bathroom. Outside, the suburbs groan but rise obedient. Taxi lights blink on and off—a new day for some, a winding down for others who see bright yolks spitting in the pan and mopped up with bread before bed, or second jobs. In town the streets are dark still but expectant; lights beneath bridges bleed into the river; the clinking chorus of steel kegs on the cobblestones. And far beyond the city, in a country field, a single ray of light slips between a crack, creeps a darkened passageway, and is greeted in a tomb by reverent gasps.

Her feet are on the floor now but the rest of her is slow to follow. Where is there to go? Without standing, she bends forward and draws the heavy drapes. The white wall flutters and sways with leaf shadows and the lighter shadows of the spaces between leaves, like some pacing piebald creature. She reaches out to pet it and it is gone.

Lute Player

There are two versions of *The Lute Player* by Caravaggio. One is in The Hermitage in St. Petersburg; the other is part of the Wildenstein Collection in New York City. In both versions, what looks like a child—doe-eyed, pink lips slightly parted, thin fingers strumming on the strings. On one of them, some fragments from a madrigal on the lute player's sheet music say: *Voi sapete ch'io v'amo. Vostra fui.* You know I love you. I was yours. The other does not.

Horizons

He was not long coming back on the boat. He called her. Poles had got there first, he said. Better the shambles you know. London is a joke. He hung up and texted her the address of the place he was staying.

She stared up at the steel door, its rusting hinges and bolts, standard delinquent scrawl, and a keyhole where a handle might ordinarily be. Shivering in the grey light, waiting for him to come down and let her in, she saw that she had not broken any of the habits she thought she had: they had only, briefly, been impractical to keep. Two men crossed the road and whistled through their fingers at another up the street. She held her handbag tight. She stood her ground as they sauntered on by.

Dark stairs led to a small flat. In the hallway, his painting rested against a wall with a couple of black bin bags, a pair of work boots, and a bicycle frame. She thought to say something but his head was already bent low and away from her, focused on his tins and rolling papers.

The painting had changed since she'd last seen it. He had introduced a middle ground with a distant mountain range, folds of auburn and vermillion shadows. Above them, clouds hovered low in a pumpkin sky—soft, curved strokes of cornflower, rose, pale lilac, lavender. If the intent had been to add depth, the effect had fallen flat. The original dark foreground dominated the eye, the bright sky imparting not perspective or a counterpoint to the darkness, but seeming torn from another painting altogether.

C'mere, he said.

She turned towards him and saw the painting sitting in the hallways of many places to come.

I read that Degas practised cloud formations with a crumpled hanky held up against a lamp, she said.

Just come here, he said.

He was stretched out on a low windowsill, smoking. In the street below, a kid balanced a football on his knee and an older youth restrained a pit bull. He offered her the dregs of the joint he was smoking.

I have to go to back to work soon.

Suit yourself, he said, and looked away down at the boys and the ball and the road and the dog. He rested his hand on her thigh and she let him so he moved it in between her legs and rubbed at her jeans with his thumb.

Don't, she said.

He arched his hips and pulled his pants down around his thighs.

I have to be back at work soon.

Please.

I can't.

Then what the fuck are you here for then?

A Light In The Darkness

They come every year, the last days of January—tall ships, passing through. So much that was sworn has already been forgotten, so much that was promised abandoned. Still, there is a chance again, at least, to wander on up to Merrion Square and take a look at Turner's watercolours, stroll through the park and make a day of it.

The paintings were known as a light in the darkness and she thought of them that way though she had never seen them. She thought of them trembling gold in their dark cabinet the year long, their whispers building to delirious song, pining for that month when light is at its lowest and they would be released. She approached them as a bright assurance, the room aglow with glass and spotlights. She had been waiting for this day too.

The shipwrecks, then, the looming cliff faces, grey-green squalls, and blue coldness of so many scenes struck her as bleak, and she moved through these paintings quickly, seeking the warm sunsets and rises of her expectations. She liked those landscapes that were mere suggestions of a thing and not too much the thing itself. She did not want detail or reality. She only wished to dissolve into the faint washes of peach and rose reflected in still waters.

Soon she had completed a circle of the room and seen everything she had come to see, glanced over the rest. It had not taken very long. She looked around to see what other people were looking at and lingering on, wondering what they were seeing that she had failed to appreciate. She did not want to leave yet, to go back out there.

Is this it? she asked, sinking and rising on the answer.

The Electric City Of Heck

Cattle stumbling their way down to the shallows. The water's coolness
Rising to meet them. Their hooves
Dry and hard against a clatter of loose stones *etc...*

Having rusted not quite closed, the sluice gate's
Cast iron lip runs with several downward streaks
Of wet sunlight *etc...*

Brushstrokes painted on a long-ago afternoon, and erased—
The strands of current drift midstream, their several
Interlocking patterns describe *etc...*

Etc. etc. etc...

*

Isn't it time I trashed such childhood memories?
Too comforting? Too prelapsarian? After all,
I live in the electric city and the electric city lives in me.
My pulse is the traffic's stop-and-go.
What I know of love and friendship
names the only streets I care for.

So...?

How come I'm helter-skeltering back to—where?

And for what?

Would I smother the weekly supermarket checkout queue in flowers,
weeds and swaying willow herb?
Scythe down a field of bankers and business magnates (row
upon sleek row baled and stacked, ready
to be recycled into something useful)?

Hardly. And yet...

Almost overnight, our city's been digitised, uploaded
to an encrypted site / Its inhabitants given new user names,
new passwords / Their histories deleted, everyone's
now making up the truth.

Beneath a touchscreen sky of low-watt urban stars
we each continue our separate journeys from

the very centre of the universe (where all our journeys start from,
especially the most personal).
We share nothing. The name for our loneliness
is self. We live for moments of recognition,
for brief communion.

*

Accelerating away from the Lockerbie bombing—
Staying a decade and more clear of the Twin Towers—
Keeping that downed Malaysian airliner a few days ahead—
Gaza, Syria, Iraq, Afghanistan and all the rest parked in a layby
for the time being. A tow-truck might be
on its way—

Same road, same destination.
Still *en route* to where we're always making for—
you, me and the memories we rely on like
outdated maps…

*

Or else, return to that slo-mo summer's afternoon?
Rebrand it: *The Electric City of Heck.*
Hashtag: *#solidground.*

We'll upgrade its farm and half-dozen cottages (built mostly
from the rubble of nearby Lochmaben Castle).
Give it a 21st century makeover.
Reformat it into:

- A glass cathedral that promises FaceTime between Man and his God of choice
- A glacier's permafrost core to slow the seasons' meltdown
- An ocean, cleansed to offer us all a second chance

Then, if all else fails—

Taking the best of what we have and the best of what we are, we'll reconfigure:

a streamlined rush of swifts that eat, sleep and mate on the wing,
never touching the Earth from here to Africa. Not angels,
but our guides into a free and trackless future—

our guides, our inspiration.

Ron Butlin

Notes on Jackson and His Dead
Hugh Fulham-McQuillan

It is astonishing how quickly he fills up a room with all those past selves. When he's been restless, you would believe the Terracotta army had crossed the sea, stomping along its quiet floor, just to surround him. His wife frequently had to free him from prisons formed from his wake, which, within the past year, had begun to manifest as fully functioning, but lifeless, reproductions, frozen in the position of his last movement: fleshy mannequins in his own image. To save time, and unnecessary worry and terror (which belonged to whom it is difficult to say), Jackson and his wife have predetermined exact patterns through their home so that he can move around without creating a dead end. He walks close to the walls of each room, taking narrow tacks into the centre if he needs to get something, say on a table. Yellow strips of tape mark Jackson's optimum paths through their house. I've noticed my assistants have started to follow these without thinking. Even I, on occasion, have felt a relief in following that tape, as if deciding where to place my feet was a burden generously lifted by those yellow Kinseological lines. I also have a piece, this one blue, attached to my elbow by Jackson's wife, a physiotherapist, to hold my tendons in such a way as to relieve me of pain when I hold the camera.

I never realised how randomly we walk, how inexact and clumsy our primary method of transportation can be. Children and the suspicious know and fight this, but even the most contained of adults will throw their legs forward without a thought beyond a final destination. For a segment of the film—I may use it as an introduction depending on its impact—I replicated Jackson's difficulties by tying a red string to my waist before strolling through a forest. (An assistant ties the other end to the car and holds it taut. Another films me from a distance.) Within minutes my possible routes are narrowed by lines of string looped around the trees. After half an hour I have painted the forest red and stand near the centre in a small clearing: about three paces squared. I had previously forbidden my assistants to rescue me until an hour had passed, so I waited, surrounded by my self-imposed, arbitrary, restrictions. The footage really makes you think, which is difficult.

Jackson tends to forget his assigned paths when angry or upset. It's fascinating how each mood corresponds to a different pattern of walking. In anger he moves in jagged zig zags, in sadness and rumination his steps take him in ever-decreasing circles until he becomes stuck in his centre. Sometimes, and this seems to be dependent on the subject of his ruminations and the speed of his steps, he creates wheels within wheels—jangly spoked bicycle wheels. In happiness he creates great looping patterns that can end anywhere. I took him out to a field where we had a camera placed on a crane. We caught marvellous images of his anger. From high enough, all those dead copies become little dark blotches—you can really understand the pattern of his mind. There are aspects of cubism there, the geometricity, the distortion—he could be an outsider modernist. I could make him that. With this strange man and his forever shedding selves as my paint, I could do that.

When he traps himself, after pacing and pacing, usually in the kitchen, until he has no way out, he has to be calm in the midst of them. I don't like their glassy stares that follow you, in that way inanimate things do so eerily, those fresh mannequins with real hair and teeth, so I have my assistants remove him. That's probably why the wife allowed us to film. She used to have to do it. I have allocated someone to take care of all that now, allowing her to return to work. I did it once. When I got through, I wasn't sure which one was him. It was like finding yourself in a room built of mirrors reflecting somebody else. It was horrible to be crowded by all those things. Jackson had to keep still at that moment. It was imperative he not move so that no more selves formed. I had to touch each one to find him. Their skins felt like hardened wax. I found him, warm and pliable, and edged the trolley under his heels, and he shuffled very slowly on to it, and I wheeled him out through his dead past, pushing them aside. It always unnerves me how light they are. They tumble if you hit them from the right angle, especially the unbalanced ones, one foot above the other in the frozen momentum of Jackson's own walk.

It really is a fantastic opportunity to capture movement in all its solid physicality. When we move there is no evidence. If someone was watching you as you stood still, then closed their eyes as you took two steps forward, in the absence of

CSI-like instruments they would have only their memory to determine that you hadn't already been standing in your new position; that a movement through space in time had occurred. The observer must trust in their memory. Jackson could never deceive anyone about his movements. His every step is documented by his old flesh. To watch him run is to see an extending diagram of a man running, each position recorded by an exact copy, with him alive at the very end of a line made of his immediate and decaying past. Old or poor recording equipment creates a blur if your subject moves too fast for the shutter. Jackson's selves make that blur physical and real. They make that reality true and make us question what we previously believed—the meaning of truth opened up like an ancient beetle, like an empty shell or flower that is more beautiful to us at night.

Their shelf date is about two days, after that... philosophy is dragged from the drawing room out to the wilderness. What is death if a man can do it so often and shuffle free each time? Death as a biological imperative, the necessity of which we have yet to discover. He dies to live. I have my assistants truck the dead selves away to the dump after a day, just to be sure. The landfill looks like the aftermath of something despicable. Note: it might make a good last scene, an aerial tracking shot revealing mountains and valleys peopled by his rotting selves: the end at the end, this is the end, death's dream kingdom etc.

We accompany him on his weekly visit to his psychiatrist. The woman is odd and, in my view, completely inefficient as a professional and, very likely, as a human. She propositioned me once, when Jackson and his wife were settling up with the secretary. She called me back and said she had always seen herself as a bohemian but her parents had made her quit painting at a young age. Then she tried to kiss me. I let her, but up close she had a sour body odour undisguised by soap or perfume. I pulled away and said I had to go. I said it quietly, looking deep into her eyes, the way you relay significant news to someone you care for, and left her wondering. I didn't mean it to, but the way I said it left me wondering a little too. Never trust a psychiatrist. She almost always presents a new pill for Jackson when we sit in her office. They are side-effect factories housed in pretty antibacterial cases. None have had any effect on his condition. They change his moods, cause gastrointestinal issues, one even coloured his skin a deep shade of orange. Seeing him walk down the road was like watching a tangerine peel itself in a slow-motion kamikaze. It might make for a humorous part of the documentary if things get a bit heavy. Note: tone.

Jackson conducted orchestras. He obviously cannot do this in his current condition—it would be illogical to have more conductors than members of the orchestra, even if those conductors are impassive lumps of flesh with only one movement—hence his fevered visits to specialists of every kind in search of treatment. I tried to get him to conduct on camera—the visual impact would be striking—something dramatic and romantic like Tchaikovsky, even the psychiatrist agreed with me on that. She is trying more and more to get me to like her since I refused her—in post-production I will enhance her efforts. Jackson has become too cowed by events to do anything like that. He mumbles, something I am told is a new characteristic of his. He says it would be a nightmare to have his orchestra see him so out of control. I have watched videos of his performances. Even with the sound down you can hear the music in his gestures, his dripping sweat and ecstasy. He is like a corpse now, apart from the eyes: all that whirlwind trapped inside those eyes. The psychiatrist believes conducting may even have a restorative effect, but he is steadfast; he is made of countless battalions.

He is cursed with an optimism redolent of an earlier age and so he doesn't allude to it, but he must be tired of so many failed explanations. It seems everyone has had a go, from specialists in physiology to readers of the future, to plain medical doctors. I've interviewed each one and will enjoy editing their nonsense and bravado. One of the more unusual—and slightly more plausible—theories came from a friend of his at the university, an assistant professor of quantum physics with hair like Medusa, if her snakes were old and tired of mythology. She suggested that every time he moved, he was in fact travelling through the multiverse, almost simultaneously inhabiting each of his infinite selves. She theorised he was the most forceful of his selves and so they grabbed on to him and landed in this dimension when he stopped moving. They cannot survive here, possibly due to the slightly altered content of our air, which may be toxic to them. They coalesce into the singular and it appears as if he is shedding a self.

I don't agree with her. Neither does Jackson's wife. She looks like an older Monica Belluci and she has a yen for continental philosophy. If Jackson dies of whatever it is that afflicts him—and we all hope he doesn't—I promise I will look after her every need. Veronica, that's his wife, thinks his problem is existential. It's to do with a lack of meaning, she says—in his search for a meaning, he is beginning to disintegrate. If he doesn't find his meaning soon, he will die a death of fragmentation. This was the first time we had a proper conversation sans cameras, assistants, Jackson. At first her words tumbled over those red velvet cushioned lips like inflexible gymnasts, but soon they stretched and then flipped into the accepting silence I had created: From the perspective of the man in the street Jackson looks like a perfect specimen, she said. I used to think he was, especially when I first played cello in his orchestra. I fell in love with that man. Now that I know him, I see that persona was about as perfectly put together as his evening wear. Beneath it he was a collection of shattered mirrors, a broken and poor imitation of a person. A mirror is not a mirror until it reflects something, otherwise it is just a piece of glass. (I'm not sure I understand this, but at the time I was swept along.) You remember when men used to only change their shirt collars and cuffs? she said, that is Jackson inside. She quoted Kierkegaard at this point (did I mention how much in love I am?):

> 'As it says in novels, he has now been happily married for several years, a forceful and enterprising man, father, and citizen, even perhaps an important man. At home in his house his servants refer to him as 'himself'. In the city he is one of the worthies. In his conduct he is a respecter of persons, or of personal appearances, and he is to all appearances a person. In Christendom he is a Christian (in exactly the same sense that in paganism he would be a pagan and in Holland a Hollander), one of the cultured Christians. The question of immortality has frequently engaged him, and on more than one occasion he has asked the priest if there is such a thing, whether one would really recognise oneself again; which for him must be a particularly pressing matter seeing that he has no self.'

She said it was only natural for a man of Jackson's immense physicality to present his sickness as a physical thing. He is dying a slow death, she said, and you are recording it for posterity. I interrupted here to assert my innocence, but she waved my words away as if she took it for granted that I was observing without helping, that that was okay. She continued: if he does not find his meaning he will die. I asked her if she believed in immortality and she said she did believe but it was of no consequence to the already-living; the self continues, but Jackson needs to find his so that he can tune into his immortal wavelength.

I could see she wouldn't be swayed from the plight of her strange husband so I let her talk some more. Then I filmed her walking through an empty playground holding an impenetrable book of philosophy. European, she said.

Note: Instead of one documentary, I could create a series, formally it would be fitting for a man with so many selves. Financially, it would be beautiful. Even if they decide to end our arrangement before I am ready, I am sure I have enough footage. My assistants film his every moment. They are closer to him as a result (Jackson has not yet spoken to me) and they report that he enjoys living on camera, that if this thing—he never names it—kills him, at least he will live on through the hours of recorded footage, previously unseen by anyone but my camera-man. I've told my assistants to encourage these thoughts of his, at least for now, for if we cannot control the end of Jackson we can control the terms of his continuation. He has recorded messages for Veronica: treatises on music, refutations of her theories, and deeply private communications that made me want to stop watching. Common to each of these is the silence that frequently envelops him. Even in the middle of sentences the words will fall away and Jackson will stare unmoving into the camera for hours at a time, like a man suddenly aware of his existence and all it entails. Then he promptly resumes his monologue—as if someone has pressed play on a video.

I'm thinking of titles: The man who carries in him a population. Jackson's search for meaning. Jackson's end. Jackson and his Dead. I like that one, it reminds me of Johnny and the Dead, which now that I try to remember I realise I cannot remember what it is about. Note: have assistants look up Johnny and the Dead before using Jackson and his Dead as a title.

FEATURED POET

Cal Doyle has read as part of Poetry Ireland's Introductions Series. Most recently his poetry has appeared in *New Eyes on the Great Book* and *The Penny Dreadful*. He regularly writes on Irish poetry for *Southword* and is the poetry editor for an online literary journal *The Weary Blues*. 'Marcus', a work of short-fiction, appeared in the anthology *30 under 30*. He is now the wrong side of thirty and is working on respective collections of poetry and prose. Cal lives in Cork, where he is completing an MA in Irish literature and cinema in UCC.

Sirens

Suggestive Sea of Flame

Dear Sir: please feel free to devour me
like you would a cupcake, or a kebab
with many trimmings. My nation is trapped
in its womb of conflict:
the sun is blackened by the souls of
our slain young men. Do you like my pictures?
I am naked just for you, prospective husband
six hundred and eleven. The moon is abundant
in its punishment. All tides have stopped,
that is, except the tide of my sex [winking emoticon]
which will drown our genitals before dawn.

Graceful Machine

My feet are exquisite: I very much need you
to nuzzle them with your handsome features
or baptise them in a bowl filled
with multi-coloured confections, like skittles
or M&Ms. My hometown is a maze.
We have a fortune teller who smells like the rain.
He cupped my naked breasts when I
was fourteen, and told me that my father
was his lover. Eat the sweets from in between my toes.
Be fluid. Later I will eat you. Do not pause.
Keep eating. It does not matter that I weep.

Electrifying Mermaid

You will find my torso to your pleasure.
I am the source of all seafarers' most vigorous
erections since *One Thousand and One Nights*
and my scales are electronic: please open the link. I wish
for you to see the currents of electricity
disarrange and multiply my erotic centre: not the 'gem'
that you seek, hooded, hidden beneath the labia, but every
single scale: I cannot swim in a straight line because of them.
Strum me like a guitar: my ecstatic spasms have killed men
larger than you. I have smashed through ceilings
and broken every brittle bone in my body.

Unholy Hour

We built cities on top of cities
sunk into forgotten plains
painted over histories

and folkish sex rituals. Their aims?
Carnivorous: blocks home many of us
and consume our cells. Again,

when it comes down to the choice
between free-love (knots
of limbs, young lips, spliffs, lust)

and navigating through shots
of searing, honey-coloured liquor
twice a year (at each equinox

as the cities continue to devour
their contents on a daily basis)
we choose during the unholy hour

amidst written words in stasis
and the cracks in the night's skies
to forget where our place is.

The Heist

and they comin' over here takin'
all our jobs and all our women
   —Contemporary Irish folk saying

They arrived in the middle of the night
in a Hi-Ace van, untaxed, uninsured,
and broke in without a sound.
They snatched Mary from her bed
and bungled her into the van's hold
right in between the minimum wage gig
at Freddie's Fish and Chips
and the twelve-hour a day cleaning job
at the local abattoir.

Imelda was perched
on top of the part-time, no love, all abuse,
glass washer cum sick mopper stint at
Barry's Bar. They were worried, Mary
and Imelda. More worrying
however, was the smile painted
on the younger lad, John.

He was sat beneath
the Barista's job at Coco's Café
where you'd be lucky to get paid
the correct wage, let alone on time.
He had enjoyed being at the mercy
of the Pole's and Nigerian's grip,
as ever since he was scooped
into the middle of a hurling pitch
by the spade of his father's hand
he has always felt like a stranger
in a strange land.

Gallows Green

the   chant   still   registers

from   Barrack Street   in the pulse

of its   stones   howls of the

condemned   contrast   against   ·

Saint   Finbarre's   spires:

a shadowplay   between   faith

and   tears, of   State and

lovers   to never   fuck

again   a   broken neck

erasing   the   taste

of   skin : *we   marched*   *up*

Gallow's   *Green*

to   *die*   *for*   *crimes*

against   *their*   *Queen*

A History of Film, Vol. 1:

Time Regained

Before we read the *mise en scene*
as a shadow of our "hero's"
lust for the girl with the lips,

a death defying grasp of Eros
and sex that rattles a car, unlike the rain,
as their bodies eclipse

the delicate arrangement in the frame:
the mole on her neck as she slips
out of her dress, the cross

tilted on the wall; through this timeless mix
of sacred and profane
the action alone transmits to us

everything they never, but need to say
to escape from the bonds of their families,
we must consider those earlier clips

                    *

which flickered onto screens
without the glitz, or the fuss
of an overheated star-system:

the down-and-up of the wall
as it sucks-in the dust
from the fabric of the waistcoats

                    *

of the erstwhile demolition crew;
the seed of narrative film

where the audience sat to face the oncoming train
and watch Time undress, frame by frame.

DERMOT HEALY (1947–2014) was one of Ireland's most admired writers. When he passed away at the end of June this year, he left behind a unique body of work that spans the full literary spectrum: fiction (four novels and one short-story collection), non-fiction (*The Bend For Home*, a memoir), five poetry collections, and nine plays.

He was a great supporter of his fellow writers. He founded and edited the literary journals, *The Drumlin* and *Force 10*, and he gave generously of his time facilitating workshops and local writers' groups in Sligo and Leitrim. We were very happy to have him as a guest speaker on our novel-writing workshop in the Irish Writers' Centre and to have had the opportunity to publish an extract from his last novel, *Long Time, No See*, in our Spring 2011 issue.

Kevin Barry's essay here is an advance printing from the forthcoming book *Dermot Healy: Writing the Sky—Critical Essays and Observations* (edited by Neil Murphy and Keith Hopper) which will be published in 2015 by Dalkey Archive Press. We are thankful to both the editors and to Kevin for permission to publish the essay.

Essay | Sligo Occult: On Dermot Healy's Radical Style

Kevin Barry

If you understand that the life of this island and its counties is permeated by strange sea-blown forces and occult shimmers, that in fact nine-tenths of the true life here lies beneath the surface of ordinary things and is utterly unexplainable, and thus beautiful, then you will understand that Dermot Healy's work feeds from this critical truth like nobody else's, and a close reading of it may help you break through to the stranger dimensions.

Witness chapter fourteen of the novel *Long Time, No See*, a sprightly twelve-page roundelay called 'Sightseeing'. It depicts a weekend night on the streets of Sligo town. Mister Psyche and his mother and father and the dog, Timmy, have driven in from their home on the coast. We understand this to be a ritual excursion. The father goes walkabout—I use the aboriginal term advisedly—and huddles in various doorways of the town as he watches the night's moves. Mister Psyche and the mother, meanwhile, sit darkly cocooned in the car down by the Tesco. They eat a few sweets and monitor the night, also. It drifts in strange eddies and turns, as though on the drag of the moon. They occasionally break off from their quiet observations to have a mooch about the streets themselves. There are random bits of chat with recurring spacers. The récit busies along on very light feet—the style is honed and fine, the authorial voice is the merest whisper of a breeze across this night and world, but listen carefully and you will hear the steady beating of a clean narrative pulse. We are presented with the surface of things—a town that is simultaneously gaudy and drab—but only as an instruction that we should try to look beneath, that we should try to go deeper. Here is Mister Psyche, having a wander around a monastery in the town, and finding that it presents a vantage view:

> I climbed the round steps up and looked down out of that V-shaped window. Underneath the souls in coats strolled in a medley. Even as they talked together, squinting to the person on their left, or right, they looked like animals entering new territory; and those who knew the place, and walked ahead through the dark with great confidence, were more alone than the strangers. I waved, but no one saw me.

Those most familiar with the terrain are most compromised by it. Great oddness might lurk in the shadows; pools of unknowable darkness might lie beyond the normal realm. But we are not going to get too het up about this; there is no hand-wringing, nor existential despair—Mister Psyche and the mother go and eat a crepe outside the cinema. The father remains in the doorways, watching the town with the bead of a hawk—if he didn't, it might disappear.

More night, more life:

> The Hill was full of Northern bucks wrapped in shawls. Three girls, dressed as barbers, were singing in the Glazed Oven. Ma bought three slices of tongue, a bag of paprika, almond nuts and yes, sage, she said. At the monument a woman was screaming into her friend's mobile. Ma strolled over to Molloy's the drapers to see the style. She passed my father who was standing outside Currid's the chemists. She did not look at him, and he did not look at her.

Chronologically we are in the present tense but also we are in the future-medieval. It is impossible to situate this work in any canon. We are neither in the dreary kitchens of social realism nor in the heritage park of late modernism. Healy is something very unexpected and rare in the literature now: he is original.

Mister Psyche and the mother are back in the car. A young one stumbles against the car in the dark. Certainly she is half-cut and we suspect that she is on tablets. She has a huge pair of eyes on her. An exchange of unmarked dialogue lowers itself by careful holds down the rockface of the page:

> We're waiting for my father.
> Oh is he doing the shopping?
> No.
> Ah, I know, he's in the pub.
> No.
> It's kinda mad. What's he doing?
> He's walking about, looking round him.
> Oh. And you just like sit … like … here?
> Is right, said Ma.
> Yes, every Saturday night.
> And Christmas Eve.
> That's weird.
> Is it?

The lines are pared to the quick and play queer music. The rhythm is not overly emphasised, being properly sprung. There is lightness, lightness on every page of the novel, and the pages turn as they should in a piece of natural art, as in the unchangeable sequence of a dream, but—ho ho—a trap is all the while being set for the reader. What we are being given here in slow reveal is another tragedy, another goat-song.

Long Time, No See is also a repository of great strangenesses. An old stone wall is recovered from beneath the sea and Mister Psyche can sense the reverb of its ancient constructor's building rhythm. There is a virtuosic set piece on the cleaning of a big house's chimney. Time is not entirely fixed—it comes and goes with the Atlantic gusts. Half the time—as in life—you wouldn't know where you are nor when. The inanimate is often enlivened:

> An empty bucket went flying across the field … A heave of salt flew across …

Land and the weather will sometimes speak; the buildings of the towns and villages hardly ever shut up. Memory seeps into the stones of our places, and it leaves us in no doubt of its lingering.

The novel sifts its material and allows it to build in slow accumulation. Dunes of quiet prose form in scimitar drifts. The bird life is in every ounce and atom as important as the human; its music is our constant grace and fills the skies:

> A choir of starlings stood feeding on the seeds of the New Zealand flax that stood over my head in the next flower garden. Hallo, I called. Hallo, they called back. Then they began the flirty whistling. A stonechat spun by, then the wren, with a tipped-up tail, hopped along a branch of olearia, keeping time to a questioning song she sang alone.

The book is utterly practical; also it is away with the faeries. Always, always it is pressing a palm lightly against the screen that shades us with a grey gauze from the Otherworld. The accent of a very particular sector of the Irish north west is delineated with precision. We listen intently to what's not being said beneath the surface of the talk. There are constant silent tussles beneath the babble of talk. In *Long Time, No See*, whenever two Irishmen say hello to each other, one of them loses.

The power of the novel accumulates, too. Slowly but definitely, and gladly, we enter the world of the book; the accent quickens, life and the night happens, and quietly a great fiction writer is at his work; the mesmeric forces assert.

Codladh

Codladh na bhfíréan a dhéanann mise.
Caitear anuas an phluideog
Agus is cnapán mé, balbhán, lúbaire, corpán,
Cráin mhór ar lár.
Taobh thiar de mo dhaillicín síoda,
Ní rinceann mo chaipíní súl.

Ach, corruair, i ngan fhios—fíbín oíche—
Preabaim, prapálaim chun turais
Ar fud m'fhearainn chlúmhaigh féin:
Rothlaím deiseal, deiseal, roileagán ró,
Is mar ungadh cosanta, tálaim sreang seile
Ó cholbha go colbha an tochta.

Nuair a dhúisím, báite agam féin,
Ní dhearmadaim ar fad na mairbh sin
A luíonn faram, scaití:
Maimeo thíos fúm ina srann agus í spíonta,
Uncail liom ag úscadh uisce a bhéil féin,
Deirfiúr liom ag castáil léi de réir na gréine.

Máirtín Coilféir

Sleep

I sleep the sleep of the just:
Once covered,
I'm a stone, struck dumb, a corpse,
A lost sow.
Behind my silk blindfold,
My eyelids won't budge.

Now and then, though,
Something takes hold:
I tour a downy world,
Clockwise, clockwise, around I go,
Dribbling a web
From south to north.

When I wake up sopping,
They're with me still,
The dead who came along:
My grandmother, half-spent,
My uncle pumping spit from his mouth,
My sister spinning with the sun.

Translated from the Irish by Martin Howard

Night Watch

That night the disappearing Mayo light
lingered long, fooled us into thinking
we were younger, still setting out
in the slow sunset of our youth.

As the sky sank into firelight
we lay lazily beneath emerging
stars, letting thoughts drift into
cosmology and the comforts of space,

watching a broad canvas of dreams
unfurl. That was the night when
your lips tasted of atomic dust,
your yellow dress a shimmering sun

and the perception of motion moved
us as we stilled; we shone easily
then, light dispersing the shadows
unaware of the dark varnish that covers us all.

Matthew Gedden

Strong
Andrew Fox

Randy, the general manager, and Agnes, the head of housekeeping, call Luis and me into the back office first thing Monday to figure out a plan for the armoires. The new ones will arrive on Wednesday morning, Randy says, but the truck to take the old ones away can't make it until Thursday afternoon. He leans against the filing cabinet, a rim of grease at the collar of his shirt. Agnes, perched on the edge of the desk, taps a lip with a big-knuckled finger.

As the two of them strategise, Luis stares into his hands, chin lolling on the chest of a brown polyester shirt three sizes bigger than mine. And when Agnes decides that the two of us should hump four floors' worth of oversized mock-rococo cabinets to the roof and cram them beneath the patio canopy, Luis ignores her, nods at Randy and says:

'Yes, boss.'

But in the elevator it's a different story.

'Goddamn it,' he says, 'have you seen those motherfuckers? They're six feet tall and three wide. They're two hundred fucking pounds.' He drives a boot into the base of the panelled door; the elevator jolts on its cable. 'Man, it wouldn't take too much more to make me really hate this dump, you know? Why don't they just bulldoze it all to hell and start again?'

'It's an institution,' I tell him, but I'm distracted with my phone: no calls.

*

The hotel, according to Randy, dates back to the beginning of the last century. Its first customers were the owners of the lumberyards upriver, whose patronage paid for canopied beds and brick hearths tall enough to stand in, whose sons held lavish dinners throughout Prohibition behind the laundry room's trick door. During the Second World War, naval officers billeted at the university marched down North King Street three times daily for meals in the tavern. And soon afterwards, travelling salesmen staged product demonstrations in their rooms until the yards all closed and there was no one left to sell to.

It was to the hotel's restaurant that I took my parents for cobb salads and whiskey sours on the weekend of freshman orientation. My mother wore a purple sweater and waterproof eye make-up, my father a ludicrous white linen jacket and a wide smile. And it was there too that I took Ashley two years later for thick steaks and strong cocktails after exams I knew I'd failed. I held her hand tightly across the table, listened to her talk about our future. Her voice was high and she could hardly sit still. That was before our sex got angry, our conversations short.

Now, I'm awake most mornings before my alarm and staring at the plastic stars constellated on Luis's living-room ceiling. I fold the *Star Wars* blanket marked with his childhood piss and work the coffee-maker that dominates the countertop in the kitchenette. Then we're in the car, Luis slurping coffee from a travel mug and singing along to the country station or the oldies station. We pull into the parking lot and punch our time cards at the door. We nod hello to the cleaning ladies hollering down their phones and to the overnight room-service guys comparing tips. And then we're in the elevator, on the floors, in the rooms, changing light bulbs or mopping tiles or rewiring the busted cable. Luis and I work well together. We are capable of talking about nothing to pass the time. But the major advantage of our kind of work is the opportunity it provides for silence.

*

The old armoires are cheap plywood boxes with particleboard backs and doors of imitation oak. I've gotten used to fielding complaints from guests about sticking drawers or misaligned hinges or splintered innards that shred cashmere sweaters to rags. They groan and wobble and threaten to split their joints as I lower them one by one on to the hand truck.

It's off-peak season, and at this hour most of the guests are busy antiquing or day-tripping out to writers' homes or the Shaker Village—but a few linger still to clear paths guiltily through piles of crumpled clothing or bed sheets or room service trays, one eye on the dresser where phones and other valuables lie exposed, the other on my scrawny shoulder blades or the strain that bulges my forearms.

'It's alright,' we tell them. 'We've got this.'

Luis steers the truck and I hold the armoires steady. We ride the elevator to the roof, where, this past summer, we used to sneak away for smokes and feel the sun dry the sweat from our backs. But now the air is as sharp as teeth and everything is the same iron grey as the sky. Luis and I collapse the patio chairs and unload the armoires beneath the canopy. I survey the space.

'Will they all fit?'

He shrugs. 'That's not my problem.'

To look at him, you'd think Luis was strong. When we met on my first day, I looked up into his black little piggy eyes and fist of a mouth, then down at the neckless spread of him—and I was scared. But these past few months, since he's taken me in and we've started to share a bathroom, I've seen the slushy hang of what I'd thought were biceps, the slabs of meat swinging from his chest, the slender legs.

By midmorning, he's sweated through two shirts and needs to take a break every few minutes to catch his breath. It gets so bad that, after lunch, I fetch him a Gatorade from the vending machine and leave him wheezing in the stairwell. My hands are red and calloused, the fingers curled towards the palms; when I try to straighten them out, the tendons ache and moan like cables.

The only way to preserve the armoires' joints is to get right under their tilting weight, and if I wedge the hand truck against a wall the work is just about doable alone. By four o'clock, I've moved nineteen to the roof and stacked them end to end. That's almost half the job, and the rest will fit if we disassemble the last couple and lay them in pieces on top. While the sun fizzles behind the flat roof of the old brewery, Luis and I sit together by the stairwell door to smoke. My head is light, my lungs clean and burning. Luis flips through a porno he's found stashed behind some paint cans, jabbing at airbrushed flesh with every turn of the page. Randy comes to check on us, tie loosened to give rolling room to a beefy neck.

'That's nice work,' he says, and Luis is quick to tell him:

'You know us, boss.'

*

My parents met Ashley a couple of times. My father liked her sundress and the way she touched his arm. He reckoned that her watch and her haircut meant she came from money. My mother never liked her. Not when Ashley and I invited the two of them for dinner to the studio apartment off campus we'd decided to share for sophomore year. And definitely not when I made the call nine months later to declare that I was neither going back to school nor coming home, but instead would stay on to work while Ashley finished studying.

After that, my mother and I didn't speak for almost a month. My father called me Thursday evenings on his way back from after-work drunk bowling to tell me over and over that he didn't agree with my decision but he respected it, that my student loans were absolutely my problem and that my mother would come around. Eventually, he brokered a truce, and now my mother and I talk on the phone every week or two. She's stopped asking me to come home. She seldom asks about work. She never asks about Ashley. I haven't told her we broke up.

*

After our shift, Luis and I head over to the Howling Owl, an off-brand Hooters by the railway tracks. He likes to sit at the belly of the horseshoe bar and pant as waitresses strut past gripping pitchers of weak beer. Me, I like the sports. The Owl has a bank of TVs near its copper ceiling that show everything from college football to ladies' synchronised diving. I can lock into the athletes' mechanical action, with Luis distracted and good company for it, and the crowd around us loud enough that I don't have to think. The hours fly by.

The place is rocking to Steve Miller Band hits and Big 10 basketball. We order a pitcher, and Luis sets to jawing with some tattooed townie about last year's hockey play-offs and about why he doesn't vote. A bachelorette party slams tequilas at my elbow. The bride wears a brittle-looking veil and the maid of honor brandishes a gummy purple dildo. Our pitcher disappears before half-time. Luis orders a second, then a third, then a basket of wings and makes it known that tonight he'll go for the title.

The record at the Owl on dollar wing night is fifty-one dollars, fifty-one wings. If you can beat that, your whole party eats and drinks for free, and they give you a T-shirt with a picture of an owl dripping buffalo sauce from its feathers, which Luis has been eyeing for months. He's been in training, conditioning his stomach. Last week, he broke forty for the first time and tonight he's feeling lucky.

He delves his hands into the carnage of the basket and pulls them out two-at-a-time. He closes his thick lips around nubs of orange flesh, sucks and gnaws and nibbles and draws out the clean, dark bone. The townie chants his name. The bachelorette party whoops and rubs his shoulders. But by thirty-seven, Luis' eyes are glassy, his forehead is red and oily and he pushes the basket away, hiccupping, belching, beaten.

At last call, he persuades one of the waitresses to slip us a bottle of gin for cash in hand. He is too drunk to drive so I take the wheel and pilot us without thinking to our summer after-hours drinking place upriver—a picnic spot with a row of rimy tables and a canopy of overhanging trees that rattle their leafless branches. The night is black but for our headlights. The air smells of frost and skunk. I sit shivering on the fender and Luis sprawls out flat on the hood. The ticking engine warms us as we pass the bottle back and forth.

I take out my phone to call Ashley. She doesn't answer. I leave a message.

'You shouldn't've done that,' Luis says once I hang up. He is silent for a long time, lips twisted in disappointment. Eventually he says, 'And you've been on my couch for long enough.'

He rolls off the hood and staggers to the riverbank. For a moment, I'm worried and half-excited that he'll tumble over the edge but he steadies himself against a tree. I hear the slap of vomit on water, the shudder of dry heaves. Luis walks back, drawing a hand across his lips, and clambers into the car.

'Just fix it with Ashley,' he says. 'Okay? You only get so many chances.'

His big head thuds against the bulkhead. I drive us home with the window open to air the stink of vomit. I hope for a deer or a raccoon to appear in my high beams, something warm and alive that I could fail to avoid. But nothing comes.

*

In the morning, a voicemail from Ashley awaits me. She, as far as I know, still gets up at 5 AM to read, and right now she'll be on her way to her work-study at the gallery. How *fine* it was, she says, to hear from me, and behind her voice I can hear the weatherman forecast a blizzard on the TV I wired into our kitchen.

I work the coffee-maker, go out to smoke but keep walking, and find myself sometime later zipping my jacket over my uniform and jogging through an iron gateway at the university's western end. At this hour, the campus is quiet: just some men from the phone company, an administrator type in a cherry-red Gore-Tex and a girl with an enormous backpack limping towards the library. Above me are the dorms, churchy grey stone piles with redbrick edging; and to the right is the concert auditorium, all swooping lines and hammered aluminium and vinyl posters of cellists. Before I flunked out I hardly ever went to class, but now I realise with a pang how long it's been since I've learned anything. I'd like to know how something works, why something is the way it is.

*

'Where the hell were you this morning?' Luis says in the locker room. He is freshly showered and clean-shaven but with nicks in his tubby jaw.

I splash water on my face at the sink and smooth the hair at the nape of my neck.

'I went for a walk,' I tell him. 'Ashley left a message.'

'Oh.' Luis checks his watch; we collect the hand truck and head for the elevators. 'Man, I don't expect she was too happy. I couldn't believe it last night when you said what you said to her.'

'Well, there's no taking back any of it now.'

The doors open on a wobbly old guy wearing an Air Force cap and oxygen tubes. Luis pushes the lobby button for him and leads us down the hallway to our first room. I knock and we announce ourselves but are greeted only with silence. Luis swipes his master key in the lock and pushes open the door. The armoire waits by the window, heavy and immobile. Luis hunkers beside it. I spread my weight, square by body and put my shoulder hard into stubborn wood.

All morning I shove and heave and blat the things on to the truck or into the carpet. We wheel the armoires to the roof and position them in clean rows like dominos ready to fall. At lunch, we choke down plates of sodden calamari left over from a Chamber of Commerce meeting. Luis reaches into his mouth and pulls out a long strip of flesh, burnt and flayed by last night's wings. I squirm in my seat, a firm nut of pain growing harder at the small of my back. Luis looks out the window at the lowering sky.

'Snow coming on,' he says.

After lunch, we switch over: I hunker to steady the truck or pin it down with a forearm when the armoire tries to tip it. Above me, more than my own weight in bargain basement cabinetry teeters and groans, and the only sign of Luis is the squeak of his hands on the veneer. In our last room, a corner joint gives way and a full side-slab shears off and falls towards me. I dive out of the way. The crash fills the room. Agnes, on one of her floor inspections, appears at the door and levels her grey eyes at us.

'Sorry,' Luis says, his cheeks flushed with hatred. 'It slipped.'

'Is that right?' Agnes says, the point of her tongue on her lip.

'That's right,' I tell her.

'Well, don't let it slip again.'

'No, Agnes,' Luis says.

We take the last armoire to the roof and break the rest of it apart. Luis kicks like a horse but I'm all frantic hands, tearing at joints and punching twisted laths and snapping pieces of particleboard until my nail beds sting with splinters. Small detonations rock my knuckles. An arc of pain crosses my wrist and streaks towards my elbow. A tack rakes the meat of my thumb, draws blood; I wipe it off. Above us, the wind has picked up and the canopy fills. It flutters empty and fills again.

*

After work, I leave Luis and go out walking. I pass the Chinese restaurant full of hollering upperclassmen, the yoghurt place and the cocktail bar where Randy goes to pretend he is somewhere else. The air reaches around my waist where my shirttail hangs and down the back of my neck where my jacket collar gapes; it numbs my lips and scrapes my throat and freezes my breath in fog.

The main road out of town has no crosswalk; I take the stone steps to an underpass lit with the flicker of a trashcan fire. Around it circle two men swaddled in overcoats and one bare-legged and shivering in a dirty hospital gown. The tunnel roof dribbles the condensation of human breath.

I climb out again at the warehouse district where, at a raw space on the corner, an exhibition opening leaks its chatter on to the sidewalk. The warehouse I'm aiming for is in the middle of the block; it is built of brown brick, single-storeyed but with lofted ceilings and tall plate windows in which a chill moon dangles. I get out of the street light and smoke some cigarettes, careful to cup my hand over the embers. In dark corners and in the coldest places, the snow has begun to stick.

When the lights go off, I cross the street to meet her as she closes up. I watch the delicate way she balances a fat bag on her shoulder and a box of files against her knee.

'You could have come in,' she says

I offer a hand to help her down the steps but she doesn't need it. Her ponytail has been severed, leaving a straight-edged bob. Her thin cheeks blanch from the chill and her small nose reddens; I want to cup the heat of my hands around her ears.

'I got your message,' I tell her. 'I wanted to see you.'

'To apologise?'

'To see you.'

'Well,' she says, 'here I am.'

The party on the corner disgorges middle-aged couples. They wear camelhair coats and broad-brimmed hats, and clog the sidewalk to air-kiss. Ashley pops the trunk and I help her load her things. Her smell is old coffee and new perfume.

'You look good,' I say.

She crosses her arms and screws her lips into the goofy appraiser's face she used to practise in front of the bathroom mirror.

'You look . . .' she says, 'the same. In fact, I think you're wearing the same exact outfit as the last time I saw you.'

'It's a uniform.' I tug at the knees of my pants. 'You've cut your hair.'

'It was time for a change.'

'It makes you look strong.'

She smiles. 'That's exactly what I wanted.'

'And you're happy?' I say. 'You're doing good work?'

'I am. I really am.'

I notice gobs of snow settled on my boot and kick them off.

'That's good, Ashley,' I say. 'That's really good.'

*

For a short time in the eighties, when business was at its worst, the hotel opened its fourth floor to residential rentals. The people who took them were mostly short-term stays: professors with a one-semester contract or the better-off students between dorms for the summer months. There were some older people too who, once their children had left and their husbands or wives passed on, sold or rented their big Colonials to free up cash and to be in town.

Mrs Kimmel made the move in her late sixties and was surprised to live for another twenty-five years. She took out her disappointment at not dying on whomever she could, insisted that the cleaning staff was stealing from her and called Luis 'Taco' until he told her that was Mexican, then did her research and called him 'Ajiaco' instead. One of my first jobs at the hotel was cleaning out her suite after she died. There were just a few items of over-laundered clothing and some old room-service plates—no books, no photos of anyone. But it wasn't the modesty or even the loneliness of her life that made an impression on me; it was how, throughout those years as her mind gave up, her body had persisted, kept moving air and blood.

I think of Mrs Kimmel as I sneak in through the staff entrance and take the stairs to the banqueting floor; as I peek into the restaurant and find it dark, cross the room and lie down behind the polished warming stations. I used to think that if my body had even half her kind of resilience, I would be okay. But as I lay my head on a folded tablecloth and curl beneath another one, I'm not so sure.

All night, the floorboards creak, branches scratch the windowpanes and the elevator cables whir. From time to time, the night porter comes and sits at the table by the big bay window to pick over stolen French fries. I hold my breath, stay perfectly still, and when he is gone I take out my phone to watch a short video I recorded a little over a year ago before everything went to hell. In it, Ashley stands in our kitchen swamped in one of my sweatshirts. She is cooking to The Supremes, her small knees bouncing. She spoons something red and steaming from a pot and offers it to the camera.

*

I wake before the breakfast service and sneak back out the staff entrance. Overnight, the snow has come on strong and now it lies in deep drifts over the parking lot. I wade downtown and back for coffee and sit with it in the locker room until Luis comes in looking rumpled. He takes his coffee without a word and leads us to the lobby to await the new armoires' arrival. Outside, city ploughs struggle to clear and salt the way.

The truck rounds the corner and skids to a halt at the forecourt. Its tires crunch and its lights blink as Luis backs it in to the goods entrance. The deliverymen, Baptiste and Kenny, have an invoice for Agnes to sign.

'This is a nice hotel,' says Baptiste, whose sinewy arms are bare even in this weather.

'Real nice,' Kenny says and whistles through a gap in his teeth.

The new armoires are built of marbled walnut and intricately carved, with brass inlays and smooth-running drawers and recessed rails for hangers. They are heavier than the old ones and their joints are more secure. Agnes has arranged for the deliverymen to stick around and help us move them to the rooms. Luis pairs off with Baptiste, and I take Kenny to the service elevator. I show him how to lock it off, how to knock politely and announce ourselves firmly at a guest room door.

In the empty rooms, Kenny roams about to eye the coffee maker and the trouser press, the shoes paired on the floor and the clothing draped on armchairs. In the occupied rooms he sticks close, follows my lead. We meet a father who doesn't break from his phone and two kids who stand dangerously close to watch us work. We meet a woman in running shorts and a varsity T-shirt, dark hair wet from the shower making her look more naked than if she wore nothing at all.

'Thanks boys,' she says as we wrestle the new armoire into its alcove, although she is no older than me and is most likely younger than Kenny.

'You're welcome ma'am,' Kenny says, eyes on his shoes, hands by his sides.

We work through lunch and long into the evening. And once the new armoires have all been put in place, Agnes gives Baptiste and Kenny her best directions back to the highway, and Randy, Luis and I take the elevator to the roof to think over how we'll dispose of the old armoires tomorrow. As we rise, I hope that the canopy legs have snapped overnight from the weight of snow. I picture half a foot fitted to the old armoires perfectly, hugging the shapes of the broken and the whole alike. But when the doors open, I see that all is as we left it. The canopy sags, its legs buckle and bend—but it holds strong yet. And beneath it, the armoires wait, clean and cold to the touch. Randy takes a broom from the stairwell and jabs it into the canopy's belly. Hunks of snow fly skyward and break apart and float in dust to the street below.

I feel as though I've come through something, though not completely and not unchanged.

There will be no fresh starts for me, I realise. But there will be starts.

Hymn to the Reckless

For my brother

Together we throw flame into orbit.
The frantic patter,
the volley, the hit.
From afar it's just stars
come down to flit.

We bend quick to the flame
and pull coals into flight
Delirious slight of hand
with a teaspoon of light
Once one caught
between my fingers and seared
and that night I wrapped
my aching hand around cold beer.

We're boozy folk heroes
performing incredible feats
craft exquisite trajectories
with arms full of heat
Look! the arc as he sends it
hurdling toward me
bending with some
eccentric choreography—

We burn.
Our power, to drag a new comet trail
across the evening
a hymn to the reckless,
so breathless it falls to earth,
the air singeing—
we smolder.
Gods of our own solstice,
and solace,
there's solace in this insane game;
in being the wild ones
who manhandle coals from the flames
and make them dance.

Oh! he catches behind the back,
he's a one-man eclipse of the sun,
lays cursive lines across your eyelids
even once you've closed them
With a tap-tap-tap it comes flying to me
oh God—I got it! Lightning quick layup,
I shot it—always skyward.

We marvel at our savage skill,
at what we've harnessed.
Sleep hard with sooty hands,
flames peel us unvarnished.

One night in the smoke
with his throat full,
he turned, stilled, confessed:
You know,
I always thought
they loved you the best.

How long has he held that
pressed tight in his palm
as it scorched him?
Brave in the dim to de-clench that fist
from the ember within;
to admit what forges us.
The gentle soul who can cast flame
to the rim of the sky.
And the ember.
Exposed to air it glows,
it catches, it dies, it passes.
Toss it here.
We'll pass it back and forth
until it's ashes.

Erin Fornoff

Mouth

While travelling
a lot changes

in one's mouth

Some people have short tongues
very short tongues

Others have long bottom jaws

Each of us has a most comfortable batch of sounds

a wet library of favourites
caged birds in the garden

My mouth wants to split itself apart, lips yes but also the hinges of my jaw as though
  looking for a tight corner to bark from

People like to ask
where did you grow up

They want to decide which of my sounds belong

Bridget Sprouls

Trolleyboy
Oliver Farry

Ireland is the same size as St Petersburg Oblast. I know this because one night after work I wasted hours on internet learning information while drinking beer and vodka, and filling our big Tia Maria ashtray, stolen by Viktor from pub in Howth, with used cigarettes. The house was empty—Evgeny was back in Russia buying cigarettes to sell and Viktor was working in the pub. I wrote information down in last year's diary I got from work but never use as diary. When I got drunk, my Cyrillic began to be loose and look like English. Ireland is the same size as St Petersburg Oblast—even for a Russian that would not mean much. Maybe I say twice the size of Estonia instead? (I learned that too on Wikipedia.) I try to tell mother on phone what size is Ireland because she worries that my life is slavery here. I tell her I cross Ireland three times in one day for my work. *Three times a day you cross country, Mischka! How many hours you work, Mischka? This is like my grandfather in time of the Emperor!* But no, mother you don't understand, it is a small country. I tell her Ireland is size of St Petersburg Oblast, but she doesn't know what size is that. She even thinks St Petersburg is in St Petersburg Oblast (everyone knows it is Russian Federal Subject). So I tell her Ireland is twice Estonia's size. Then she understands a little.

It is Friday and it is the last train. It pulls out slowly of Connolly Station, crawls past the backyards of grey houses and past the big stadium that is too big for those houses. Many people will get off at Maynooth. These are serious people who work in Dublin and they are called commuters. The train is quiet while they are here. It is as if they are still working. Even when they talk into mobile phones to tell wife or husband they will be home in twenty minutes, they sound like they are arranging meeting or giving orders to unimportant workers. Most get off at Maynooth and their places are taken by students with rucksacks full of dirty clothes. That's what Marty says. When the commuters are gone, the train is different and louder. Irish country people are comical—they talk high and fast, like cockerels in cartoons. Many of these Irish muzhlans want to be your friend.

Trolley service begins when train has left the city. First customer is old lady who asks me what happened to Fintan. It is often they ask about Fintan. I say Fintan find better job as waiter in Abbey Street restaurant. *Fair play to him*, old lady says, *he was very nice, Fintan*. I serve them tea—it's always tea—taken with milk and sugar, like the English do. Fintan used to say to them, *do you want any sugar with that? Ah no, sure you're sweet enough*. Babushkas like that. But I cannot do as Fintan does. His words are not mine. My way of doing things is different. *And where are you from yourself?* she ask me. From Russia, yourself says. There was time I said Poland, until Evgeny's immigration lawyer made our papers better. *Russia!* the old lady says. *It must be fierce cold there at the minute.* No, it is not so cold now because it is spring, but yes, in winter it is cold. I have this conversation many times as I cross country three times a day. When you tell them you are from Russia they have one or two things they can talk about. Not much. Sometimes they talk about chess, sometimes about communism, sometimes great Russian writers Tolstoy and Turgenev. Once two gays talked about the Bolshoi and Kirov ballet— *oh how we* loved *the Bolshoi when they came to Dublin!*—and other time a young man surprised me and said he was big fan of Sergei Fyodorov, hockey-with-shayboy player. But the Irish know not much about Russia. Such a big country but so far away for them. Russia is not exactly next door.

Would you have any wagon wheels? says man with bad breath. I do not know if this is joke order people make in train wagons, like request colleagues made first day I worked as kitchen porter in Dublin, where I get them rubber nails or bucket of steam. I am unsure so I say no. Politely. I call him sir. Later, I must remember to ask Marty if wagon wheel is legitimate request. Man is disappointed. *They're wild difficult to find anywhere these days, those wagon wheels. I wonder why that is?* He takes Mars bar and pack of Tayto instead. And cup of tea. It is always tea, never coffee.

It is Friday and there are many students who go home for weekend. There are many girls. Irish girls are sometimes pretty but they are often fat. I have talked to some. They are not interested in Russian men, I think. *Ah, go on, give us a smile, would you?* I smile for my friends, young lady. My English is good but talk to a girl in English is a different story. I had sex with four women since I came to Ireland—one Lithuanian (half Russian), two Frenchwomen and one Brazilian. Never an Irish. I tried but they don't seem interested. The younger women on the train don't ask where I'm from. Only the older ones. The Irish babushkas are impressed by other lands. For the younger ones, it is different. They have already met foreigners and they don't care about more that they meet. My mother asks me on telephone what are Irish women like (she worries I will marry and never come back). I tell her I don't understand them. *Is it the dialect they speak, Mischka? I knew you should have gone to England instead!* No, I don't mean it like that, mother. But I know she is happy that I don't understand Irish women.

I finish trolley first service by time we get to Mullingar, which is longest time we go without station. I like to be free when train goes past lake after Mullingar. It goes by so close it feels you are sailing through the water. And then it is time for break at Mostrim, where the train waits. This is how I make my day shorter.

We stop for five minutes in Mostrim (also called Edgeworthstown but it is too long for me to say) to wait for train in other direction because there is only one line between Dublin and Sligo. I can step onto platform and have cigarette. Regulations say I cannot smoke while wearing uniform but some rules Irish don't care about. Stepping out of train to smoke is sufficient. Irish colleagues, Marty, Peter and Assumpta the conductors, always step outside to smoke. In uniform. Stationmaster of Mostrim, Mr Donlon, smokes too. In fact I have never seen him without cigarette in his mouth. The Irish have a very sensible attitude to this rule and I applaud them. Most rules they care about very much but smoking in uniform is no big deal. They know that. My cigarettes come from Evgeny, and when he cannot go to Russia so much in case Customs get suspicious, from Sergei, an Uzbek with Russian passport, who always has smokes to sell. It is impossible to smoke with Irish prices. None are cheap. I tried rolling tobacco but I am lazy. And I always forget to roll cigarette before train stops in Mostrim. The train arrives in station after five minutes. Passengers on both trains look bored. Passengers on trains always look bored when you see them from the outside. That is something I have noticed. I crush my cigarette with foot and step back onto the train when mobile buzzes in my pocket. It is text message from Viktor:

Евгений поймали. В аэропорту. Отправляясь в Москву.

I will not be able to call Viktor until train stops in Sligo.

Two euros fifty for a cup of tea? Jesus, CIE knows how to make money, I can tell you. Perhaps you should tell CIE your problem, sir. I only work the trolley. I do not set prices. I do not say this—I would get fired—but I think it. The Irish complain about money a lot but they also like money. Irish people I meet—mostly through Viktor, who has friends from pub in Howth—complain about price of everything: drink, food, petrol, car, house. But do they want their country to be poor again? It was poor. I know that (I also find out this information on Wikipedia—English version, Russian page is not so detailed). You can buy house in Tula, Kazan,

Novgorod for little money. But foreigners don't come to Tula, Kazan or Novgorod to look for job, except maybe you are Chechen or Uzbek. Sometimes I think Irish do not understand capitalism. CIE charge you two euros fifty for tea, sir, because when you step on train, demand goes up and supply comes down. Train is not outside world. This is capitalism. You don't like, you live in Cuba. It is also weak to complain about trifle things. It is weak to complain about your tea costing two euros fifty, sir. And you do not have to buy that tea, sir. We do not stick gun to your head to make you buy this tea. But I say nothing because I would get fired. I smile at customer, serve him steaming Lyon's tea in plastic cup and give him change, two euros fifty from five-euro note. He will enjoy this tea more than all other teas.

When I pass between carriage I send Viktor text:

Правда?

But customers are mostly OK. The only times customers give me trouble is when there is football match. Football fans always make jokes about you that you can't understand. The Irish football fans, even bad boys like the Shamrock ones, aren't scary like football fans in Russia do but still they are many and you are one. They call me Ivan. *Eye-van.* All Russians are Ivan to them. Ivan is my patronymic but it would be waste of time explaining patronymic to Irish people. They don't know. It is also waste of time telling them my name is Mikhail. Why must they know my name anyway?

Some days I tell them I am from Slovakia or Bulgaria, like how I said I was from Poland before I get better papers. They can't tell and they know even less about those countries than I do. They stop talking quickly. Maybe I should be Slovakian or Bulgarian all the time? But it is hard for a Russian not to be Russian. I should not betray my country like that, by pretending to be someone from a small country that Russia once ruled. Russia is not powerful like it was but it is still a great country. Slovakia and Bulgaria are not. They are more like Ireland.

I have other text from Viktor. It has more information. Yes, it is true that customs stop Evgeny at Dublin airport, they find suitcase full of cigarettes and send him back to Moscow. His better papers no help. I will call Viktor when train stops in Sligo.

I cross Ireland three times a day but I have not been to many parts of Ireland. (OK, I cross Ireland twice some days, three times other days. We have system where we work two trains three days, three trains two days and stay overnight at other end. And next week we do opposite. It works out that we don't work too many hours that way. But I am boring you.) Most of Ireland I have travelled is two metres wide. The rest of the country I know is the landscape I see from the train (very flat and pretty and flooded in winter), the platform in Mostrim where I smoke in uniform and Sligo, where the train stops.

Cheer up, it might never happen. Woman who buys Danish pastry and tea between Dromod and Carrick-on-Shannon says that to me. She has kind face but doesn't look kind when she says it. I do not know what is *it*. I cannot cheer up. I am not professional clown. And her prophecy is wrong. It has happened. Evgeny is not coming back. He will now stay in Russia. In the house in distant Dublin suburb of Rush, his belongings will remain—not much, suitcase of clothes, PlayStation, the trance CDs he burned before he left Russia. Maybe I will bring them to him when I go to Russia next. Consequences of his banishment are several: we must find new person to live in house—otherwise we pay more rent every month. It is difficult because Rush is distant suburb and many people do not want to live there. Many people do not want to live with Russians, I have found. They think: loud music, drunk on vodka and Mafia. But we prefer to have a Russian anyway because we can speak Russian in house. Other consequence: I must go to Sergei always for cigarettes now. Maybe Sergei will put up prices if he knows Evgeny is sent back to Russia. The sly Uzbek. Lady who says it might never happen is wrong. It has happened. Why do people say things like that? How does she know?

I finish trolley second service just before Ballymote, where people get off in the dark. There are still students on the train but it is quieter again. Viktor sends me another text. Why cannot he wait till I call him in Sligo? I step between carriage and read text. It says Evgeny owed money to Ukrainians in Dublin and they know where we live. I think of possibility of Evgeny sending us money by Western Union so that we can pay them but where will Evgeny get money if he has no cigarettes to sell? These Ukrainians are not nice people, says Viktor's text.

Company puts me in hotel beside the big stone station in Sligo every time I must spend the night there. Great Southern Hotel, which I find confusing, because Sligo is in the north. Sligo is small and windy. It rains a lot and the wind blows from the Atlantic Ocean, meaning umbrella is pointless in such a climate. Nothing happens in Sligo—it is much too small—but it is pleasant. Men look bigger and less shaped than in Dublin—it is more like Russia. Tonight there is a wedding in the function room on ground floor of hotel. Red-faced men in suits stand outside, smoking, with pints of flat beer in their hands. They joke with one another. It is a wedding so there is only time to have fun. Every few minutes, the door opens and you can hear music rise up and the voice of an excited DJ who talks too much.

I call Viktor from hotel. His voice is the voice of fear. He panics. *Obrechennye! We're fucked, Mikhail. They know where we live, who we are. You must steal all the money from the trolley. As often as you can. These men are bad boys. They don't joke.* This of course is an absurdity. I cannot steal all the money from the trolley. And even if I did, it is not much. Not even the fat Irish eat enough muffins and Taytos and drink enough tea and cider to make trolley takings enough. I would have to steal from trolley ten times to make up this money. I tell Viktor calm down. I will talk to Evgeny. Also, we have time. I have nine hundred euros savings. Enough for Ryanair flight to Riga for both of us and then train home. *They'll find us in Russia, Mischka!* No they won't, Viktor.

But it is hard to talk to Viktor now. He is not being rational. Viktor is allowing his fear to dominate his whole being. It would appear he is correct to be scared— these Ukrainians are not nice people. I believe him. I am scared too. But one must not be too scared. Too scared and you become an orphaned bear with sore foot, alone in the world and more danger to yourself than to anyone else. This I learned from my mother but it does not appear that Viktor had someone to tell him this. Viktor is a swarm of fear, regret, anger and irrational thinking.

I walk around the hotel room when I talk to Viktor because the matter seems too important to sit on bed. *We don't have much time, Mischka,* Viktor tells me. Yes, I know that. *I want to leave Ireland tomorrow.* No, you will wait for me, Viktor. Just leave the house if you are uncomfortable being there tonight. Go stay with friends. Make up story about house being flooded or something, I tell him. He talks about these Ukrainians and what they will do, their reputation among the cigarette smugglers of Dublin. I open window of hotel so I can have smoke. I am still listening to him. I grip mobile phone between my cheek and shoulder while I open new box of cigarettes, causing Viktor's voice to go distant for a moment. The wedding continues down below, two floors down. The country men in suits, their ties loosened, talk about football and nothing. Occasionally a woman in fancy outfit will join them for a smoke and chatter in her cartoon-cockerel voice. From inside there is still music. Muzhlan music that is loud, fast and uncultivated. Music you never hear on the radio in Dublin. *Okay, Mischka, I will go stay in town with the Serbs. I cannot believe you are being so calm. These Ukrainians do not joke.* Good night, Viktor, I will talk to you tomorrow.

After talking on phone to Viktor for so long, kitchen in hotel is closed. It is too late to eat. Also I ate only cheese bap on the train. So I go out to get curry chips in Four Lanterns, which I like. There has been rain in Sligo and the streets are shiny black. Streets are quiet. Train goes back to Dublin first thing in the morning and then I am off till Tuesday. This will be my last time in Sligo. I know it. There will not be time to hand in notice. We will fly on Sunday morning. The Ukrainians won't come looking for Evgeny until Monday, unless he was so idiot to call them from Russia. Viktor will stay in apartment of Serbian friends on the quays till Sunday. He will take all his belongings and not return to the house before he leaves.

I eat my curry chips in the bright takeaway. There are teenagers in tracksuits with bad haircuts standing around the counter talking to the girl working there. I find them hard to understand. I have seen them here before. They are too young for pubs but too old for sitting at home on Friday night so they spend time in takeaway, standing and sitting for hours, eating nothing, yapping to each other in their impossible accents. They look at me when I order my curry chips but they probably think I am Polish. They have seen many Poles before so they lose interest. I sit alone in the corner eating. It is my last time ever to be in Sligo. I have not counted how many times I have been to Sligo but I know it is more than most Irish people have been. Some Irish people may never have been there. I could say that I am a Sligo expert, though I will have to consult Wikipedia to find out more information. I will never see Sligo again so I will tonight get drunk. I will go to all the pubs I like, places that Marty first brought me to. Places that are dark, wooden, old like Soviet times. Old pubs with furniture from old churches and ruined houses. Pubs that still smell of smoke even after the smoking ban. I will not see Marty again. Sometimes I stay with him in Sligo if we are both working on the same train but this weekend he is in Canary Islands with his family on Easter holiday. I will have no chance to say goodbye, or ask about wagon wheels. I could get so drunk I not go into work tomorrow but that would be stupid as train brings me back to Dublin anyway. There is still a reason to do things right. The Ukrainians don't joke, says Viktor. Neither do I.

My mother asks me every time I telephone when I come back to Russia. I say I wait another year. *Another year! Next year, it will be another year too. I am getting old!* But mothers are like that. I would stay in Ireland, another year. Maybe another year next year too. There is not much for me in Ireland. I have trolley job on train that pays enough. Nobody pretends they love being trolley boy. But what can I do in Russia? I have no education and I have already done army. I will get job in government office where I will stamp people's forms, type information into computer and make people miserable when I tell them there is nothing I can do for them because those are the rules. And to get this job, mother will pay official 25,000, maybe 30,000, roubles, as a token of appreciation. So I can make people miserable. Right now I prefer to make people miserable when I tell them tea costs two euros fifty. It is easier to make such people miserable because to complain so strongly about tea one must already be miserable at heart. That is something I have noticed.

For The Time Being

Oh strange party of the heart. Who in that living room
was what we call alive? Mother
was dead of course, that's why we were
at her friend Laura's party, Laura who said, *Her obituary is*
perfect, except for one word—you described

your parents' wartime romance as a whirlwind,
but your mother told me their courtship was
torrid. Strange heartfelt party where somnambulists
who felt like weeping instead placed bets
on whatever might blaze fastest.

In postwar Paris, Laura passed a gallery each evening
and longed for the Modigliani in the window.
One bereft day it was gone. Then finding it was
only being cleaned, she gambled everything she had
and made an offer. Modigliani, the spectacular, the impossible

man, who had TB by sixteen and knew his only chance
was *a brief but intense life.*
And out of the wreckage he made of that knowledge,
out of absinthe, out of poverty, out of hashish,
out of treating those he loved

terribly, came this serene portrait, a young Polish émigrée,
head at a slight tilt,
nose long and curving as a Byzantine Madonna's,
piled-up dark hair just beginning to unravel
above a small, colorful smile. *Sixty-three years*

she's traveled with me, Laura told my father. *Almost as long*
as you and Alice were married.
Laura's gone now, the painting is journeying someplace new,
and I'm told that Laura's friend at the party, Hana,
has also died. Hearing Hana was from Prague

Dad said, *Lovely city! I was there once,* then stopped
himself, realizing it wasn't part of his grand tour—
he'd seen it from the air, seen it beneath flak and flames.
So many ghosts, even at the most recent parties.
Under the Polish woman's portrait, the taste of mint

and strong, sweet juleps, Mother at the center of things,
my father smiling on the edge of tears, and the horses burst
from their floodgates, colors surging above a wet-fast track,
all of us hovering between a hush and a shout,
and it's the horse so far back its jockey couldn't see

the rest of the field, the 50-to-1 gelding that charged the rail
so quickly the announcer missed him till he was three lengths clear—
a spectacular upset, an impossible
result! Mother, after twelve days of sleepwalking we wake
to find ourselves applauding a jockey with a Cajun accent

who tosses a rose to the sky, the son who left school after ninth grade
but promised his parents he would amount to something,
and in this party going on in my heart
where some of us are dead and the rest will follow soon enough
everyone for the time

being is singing, and the words go, *Weep no more, my lady*—
None of us picked the winner, but we're cheering
the horse from nowhere,
we're throwing our brief intense roses
into the waiting air—

Ted Deppe

Breadwinners

I was seven
when my mother told me
I was a store-bought loaf of bread.

You know in countries like Afghanistan,
the Taliban clear out towns by killing bakers.
People starve. But this is America,
and here we never know who makes our bread.
Our bakers are never considered precious.

She let me read my recipe.
I was missing ingredients, but
I got the point.
130 grams of water,
and the same amount of all-purpose flour
with fast acting yeast
(the rapid-rise kind).

She and my father planted their own wheat seeds,
most didn't take.
The others were only good for cake flour,
and they needed bread.

So they bought me from a baker.
I never met her, but she fed my leaven
adding unequal parts of flour and water.
Rubbing her knuckles through me
sweating, making work of the thing.
Her heart pounding as she created mine
letting me sit a few minutes
before folding me over myself
on a stone to cook.

After an hour she turned me onto my belly
so I would bake evenly through.
She probably even sang to me while I rested and rose,
finally making several symmetrical slashes on my back
before serving me up to my parents.

Jillian Kring

That Quiet Entanglement

That light makes remarkable
shapes in the night. That glow that
seeps through the crack of the door.
That shine that glimmers slightly
against the corner of that
white wall where that picture hangs.
That picture you drew of me
in that black hoodie. Ever
so gently that pencil stroked
the page and the pencil shades
an image you have of me—
that song in my mind that you
sang so quietly that night
your toes grazed my shins so we
looked up as the light shone in.

Jillian Kring

Finishing Touch

Claire-Louise Bennett

I think I'm going to throw a little party. A perfectly arranged but low-key soiree. I have so many glasses after all. And it is so nice in here, after all. And there'll be plenty of places for people to sit now that I've brought down the ottoman—and in fact if I came here for a party on the ottoman is exactly where I'd want to sit—I'd want to sit there, on the ottoman. But I suppose I'd arrive a little later on and somebody else would already be sitting upon the ottoman very comfortably, holding a full glass most likely and talking to someone standing up, someone also holding a full glass of wine, and so I would stand with my fingertips upright on a table perhaps, which wouldn't be so bad, and, anyway, people move about, but, all the same, I would not wish to make it very plain just how much I'd like to sit there, on the ottoman—I certainly wouldn't make a beeline for it!—no, I'd have to dawdle in and perch upon any number of places before I'd dare go near it, so that, when finally I did come to sit on the ottoman, it would appear perfectly natural, just as if I'd ended up there with no effort or design at all.

Howsoever, I am not, and never can be, a guest here, though in fact taking up the rugs and changing everything around and putting the glasses in a new place—two new places actually, there are that many glasses—does make it all quite new to me, and I have stood here and there sort of wondering what it was all for, all this rearranging, and it seems to me I must be very determined—it seems to me my mind is quite made up about who's in and who's out. With everything changed and in new places I can say to myself, no one has been here yet—and now, I get a chance to choose, all over again—I must be very determined after all, to make things fresh and stay on guard this time. Yes, I get a chance to choose all over again, and so why not make use of such an opportunity in a very delightful way and throw a little party, because it is perfectly clear to me now who I will invite and who will not know a thing about it—until after perhaps, there might be some people who were not invited who might come to know a thing or two about it afterwards.

And that's just fine, that's fine by me. After all, isn't a party a splendid thing not only because of the people there but also because of the people who aren't and who suppose they ought to be? No doubt about it, there'll be a moment, in the bathroom most likely—which will naturally exude a fresh and subtle fragrance because of the flowers I picked earlier from the garden—when I feel quite triumphant for having developed the good sense at last to realise that people who are hell bent upon getting to the bottom of you are not the sort you want around. This is my house—it doesn't have any curtains and half the time half the door is open, that's true. The neighbour's dog comes in, that's true too, and so do flies and bees, and even birds sometimes—but nobody ought to get the wrong idea—nobody ought to just turn up and stick a nose in! I wonder if it'll become wild or whether people will stay in range of tomorrow and leave all of a sudden around midnight. I wonder actually if anyone will ask what the party is for. Because of the summer I'll say. It's because of the summer—this house is very nice in the summer—and that'll be quite evident to anyone who asks. Yes! It's for the summer, I'll say, and that'll take care of it.

And sure enough there'll be martinis and Campari and champagne and bottle after bottle of something lovely from Vinsobres. And beautiful heaps of salad in huge beautiful bowls. Fennel and grapefruit and walnuts and feta cheese and all kinds of spread-eagled leaves basking in oil and vinegar. Because of the summer! Can't you see! No doubt there'll be some people who will be curious and will want to take a look upstairs—and perhaps I won't mind at all but I shan't go with them unless, unless—no, I shan't go with them no matter who they are. Sure, I'll say, over my shoulder, go on up and take a look. Be my guest. And then, not long after they've come down and made this or that comment, I'll find some reason to go on up there myself—I won't be able to help myself—I'll want to try to see what it is they saw I suppose and maybe I'll get quite the shock when I discover just how revealing it is up there. I wonder who out of everyone will sit on the ottoman? Well if you must know that is not a spontaneous point of curiosity and I don't wonder really because in fact I already possess a good idea—a clear picture actually—of who will sit upon the ottoman. Oh yes, a lovely picture as clear as can be. And as a matter fact it might be the case that this vision preceded my fantasies about being a guest here myself and artlessly contriving to sit on the ottoman beneath the mirror—I'd go further and say the vision, the premonition if you will, of who exactly will sit on the ottoman very much instigated my fantasy of doing just the identical thing. What kind of a calamity would it now be if as it turned out the person I have very much in mind does not in fact sit upon the ottoman but leans in the doorway, for example? Just leans against the door frame and picks at the door jamb, actually. Would it appear so very eccentric if I suggested to them that in fact the ottoman is a very nice place to sit? Well of course it would, it would be very eccentric, and my friend, and by the way I don't even have this woman's phone number, would understandably feel a little unnerved that I'd singled her out in this way—in this strangely intimate way. Of course I could devise some kind of game that included everybody and involved me appointing each person a place in the room—that could work—that would work—but it would be stupid, even if they thought it was sort of charming and zany I would know it was absolutely bogus and stupid, and how would I live with myself for the rest of the night after that exactly? Still, despite all that, despite how fraught this can all become, I am quite unperturbed—I'm determined you see, quite determined to host a low-key, but impeccably conceived, soiree.

I don't mind asking people to bring things by the way—and I'm very specific. Gone are the days when I make a lot of work for myself—that might surprise you, it surprises me. I'm very forthright on this matter, which is something people appreciate very much in fact because, naturally, people are short on time and they can't allocate time to trying to work things out like what to bring to other people's parties, it's a minefield, and even if you do have time to give to working such things out the fact is there is always an anxiety that what you finally select to bring is a real clanger. It never is a clanger, not really, but who wants to sit in the back of a cab with a bowl covered with tin foil in their lap wondering if what it contains is going to be met with melodious condescension—who needs any of that? Give people a specific request and they arrive feeling pretty slick and raring to go. Not that the requests are issued in haphazard fashion of course—I know perfectly well who to ask to supply the cheese for example, and who to contribute the bread. It's easy to notice what people enjoy eating, and from there it's reasonable to infer that they'll endeavour to procure the finest examples of whatever comestible treat it is they have cultivated a particular fancy for. And, naturally, there'll be one or two you let off, simply because, gusto notwithstanding, they've never demonstrated any discriminating interest in what they eat. They'll probably rock up with hash and breadsticks, and quite possibly a dim jar of drilled out green olives, and people who stay late will horse into the breadsticks and the following day there'll be shards of breadstick all over the floor, ground to a powder in places, where people have stood on the bigger shards while talking to people they don't usually talk to, or even when dancing about perhaps. I always enjoy the day after in fact. Slowly going over everything from the night before until it's all just so. Everything in its place; awakened, accomplished and vigilant.

As it turned out he came and she didn't. They couldn't get a babysitter you see. He came on his bicycle and his face was incredibly flushed, which he seemed to be enjoying very much. Indeed, it is nice to be flushed, whatever way it happens. I can't recall what he bought with him, which surprises me—I've a feeling it was something that needed to be kept flat because I seem to remember that the minute he came in the door he was anxious to look inside his rucksack. It was a tarte, I remember now. From the gourmet bakery near the canal. That's right, he took a tarte normande from his rucksack and it was perfectly intact—and there was a bottle of Austrian white wine too with a distinctive neck which I put in the fridge right away and I don't think I opened it until much later on—the neck was distinctive you see and I remember putting my hand around it again quite late, it was really chilled, possibly too much. There was lots of wine, more than enough, and I was pleased about that, in addition my friend with tenure brought beer and a bottle of my favourite gin, which was unexpected and very kind because that particular gin is astronomically expensive. Everyone came with something thoughtful in fact and now and then I'd bring some chicken wings out of the kitchen, or one of those pizzas that have such beautifully thin bases some people presume they're home-made, and everyone already knew each other so I could do whatever I liked and didn't have to worry about whether so-and-so was enjoying themselves because anytime I looked around there wasn't anyone who looked left out, but then it's so small in here it would be pretty difficult for anyone to look left out even if they felt it.

For a long time a man sat on the ottoman, I don't remember which man and perhaps it alternated. I just remember jeans and boots, and of course that wasn't at all what I'd had in mind. Quite often I'm terribly disappointed by how things turn out, but that's often my own fault for the simple reason that I'm too quick to conclude that things have turned out as fully as it is possible for them to turn, when in fact, quite often, they are still on the turn and have some way to go until they have turned out all the way. As my friend who lives nearby frequently reminds me, that part hasn't been revealed yet. My fascination was short-lived in any case, perhaps it lasted a fortnight, less, and it was only brought about in the first place by a blouse she wore one day—the collar, to be precise. The way her head was bowed, actually, just above the collar. So that you could see the roots of her hair, which was parted and pulled back. She was flipping through a very thick fashion magazine. One hand flipped through the magazine and the other hand was up near her face—near her chin—near her collar. What must it be like, I thought, to stand there like that, flipping through a fashion magazine? That shows you how determined I was, how utterly determined, to overhaul everything, to convince myself anything at all was possible—and obviously I must have thought that it must feel really terrific, standing there like that, flipping through a fashion magazine, wearing discreet earrings and a diaphanous collar. Well really, I get so carried away.

The following day I took my time and returned everything gradually. There were lots of crackers and grapes left over, and some nicely subsiding cheese. In fact I discovered all sorts of things here and there. Including a small bag of jelly babies on the windowsill. There's bed linen inside the ottoman by the way—some of which I've had for years.

Autumn

It is autumn again
and I'm not ready.

Handy then
that you should give me

this scrap of hessian, the *rough,*
dumb country stuff that I adhere to.

Whoever stitched it
sews as I do,

with an uneven hand,
with the understanding

that even torn things
may be patched together.

I need this flint arrowhead
for there's flesh to be cut from old wounds,

and now the cold
has come again

I'll take this button
for my coat—

its pockets may be empty
but into the lining

I have sewn
a minute envelope.

It holds the twenty-six letters
of the alphabet

and one full-stop;
potent as a bullet

or a kiss.

Grace Wells

Pomegranate

The first was September, late sun,
sudden loss.

October brought a language of decay,
mushrooms, lichen, liver-spots on her skin.

She swallowed, and birthed November—
grey month of continual rain.

And sucking the next seed, she sucked light
from the sky, let night conquer December.

Not a winged insect alive on the air,
she created a January so raw it engendered courage.

She put another in her mouth
and set free the sharp frosts of February—

how bittersweet the pips, their ruby flesh
so sensuous, the white seed tart and bitter.

She smiled and winced,
tears in her eyes,

eyes watering in the March wind,
her lips stained with sugar.

Grace Wells

First Kiss

He kissed me quite by surprise.
I could feel his mean little smile
as he turned from the passenger window,
swung his face to mine,
a half-moon hooked in his hair.
The streetlights fluttered,
his reptile tongue
shot out like an arrow
and everywhere, I felt him—

my stomach sucked in
below a staircase of rib
rising to meet full flesh, these breasts
the colour of yesterday's milk.
His hands, I remember, were warm,
having already trapped them
beneath denimed thighs
for the whole small-talking journey
and outside through the still window
the shadow of somebody's childhood
ran laughing away to the moon.
Turning slyly, adder-eyed,
his palm coasted my pelvic bone,
pressed his thumbs to the hipped sockets.
Kissing me for the first time,
even the stars were nothing more
than a flicker you just got used to.

Natalie Holborrow

Bittersweet Nightshade

Frank Schulz
Translated from the German by Rachel McNicholl

The yellow crowns of the maples gleam, though the sky above Poppenbüttel looks like an X-rayed rib cage. The long Indian summer had come to an end the day Lothar went off to Bad Kissingen. Dörchen scuffles with her feet to make the leaves rustle. She had polished her shoes before she set out, but ever since the business with the savings club and the matchbook she has kind of lost interest. The scent of compost, peat-mould and leather wafting up reminds her of the red wine Gitti treated her to after they'd dropped Lothar off at the Hauptbahnhof. 'Pretty bitter, isn't it,' said Dörchen after the first mouthful, and Gitti said, 'You just don't know what's good and what isn't.' 'Yeah, yeah,' said Dörchen, 'Your silly old mother knows nothin',' and Gitti rolled her eyes, and Jeannette said to Gitti, 'Leave Granny alone', and gave Dörchen a kiss.

To get to the S-Bahn platform, Dörchen has to negotiate a set of steps. Her heart races from the effort but has settled, more or less, by the time the train pulls in. As long as she doesn't think about the matchbook in her handbag, her pulse stays steady during the train-ride too, more or less. But it starts up again when she has to change trains, and after hauling herself up the steps to the Reeperbahn, the blood is pounding so hard in her neck that she has to loosen her silk scarf and lean on the railing to catch her breath. She has kind of lost interest since that business with the savings club and the matchbook—but only kind of: Dörchen has no intention of giving up. The same Dörchen Possehl has never given up, not in winter 1961, when she pushed Gitti out of a very wayward position into this world; nor in the 1970s, when Lothar's double shifts of schnaps and beer chasers got out of hand; nor when Günni had that awful accident away on military service; not even that time she nearly lost the will to live, after the tick bite in Tyrol.

Lothar had worked for a construction company for forty years, and even though he was retired, they'd invited him to their big anniversary bash. After the official party, he had gone off down the Reeperbahn with a few former workmates. Like

Dörchen now, Lothar hadn't been in St Pauli for the best part of thirty years. Whenever they had visitors from Sauerland or Munich, they would take them on a boat trip round the Alster or the harbour, to the zoo or maybe the Fish Market. Strange, all the people around here nowadays. She fumbles in her handbag for the matchbook, checks the address again and battles her way up the street; the oncoming stream of people parts around her or stalls, only to break up and flow on, brushing her trench coat in passing; twice someone barges into her. The chatter and laughter, the roar of four-lane traffic and the raunchy repartee of the barkers rush right through Dörchen's head. She's only got eyes for the numbers on the buildings and, one hand on her hat as she looks up, the signage above them; she filters out all the multi-coloured posters in the windows, all the neon tube-lights flashing on cornices, the blacklight pillars, the pools of ultraviolet light in the entrances, and eventually she finds what she was looking for. There it is, in the same sweeping, luminous red script as on the matchbook: Moulin Rouge.

Stationed one step in front of the entrance lobby, a stout woman is twirling a sort of majorette's mace. She's wearing a porter's uniform, a low top hat and unreal make-up. 'Hello, love. Lost yer way?'

'No, I just want…'

'Hey, ye old rockers!' the doorwoman suddenly bawls over the feather on Dörchen's hat, shoving her to one side. 'Come on in! Get a load off! Get yer nuts off!' She taps one of the group with her mace, as if to put him under a spell, and behind her back Dörchen darts into the vestibule, gets caught in the heavy door-curtain but untangles herself again.

Inside it's as warm as a henhouse. The walls of the lounge are papered with red brocade. To the right and on the far side, booths for two are separated by curtains in old rose. It's quite nice, really. Almost like the Tivoli, back in the day. Funny she should think of that now. Dörchen heads for the first of the booths. Two banquettes, a low balustrade supporting ledges for drinks, on each ledge a parchment-shaded table lamp, a glass of paper-wrapped straws, a holder with a drinks list, a clean ashtray on a paper coaster. And in the ashtray an identical matchbook to the one in Dörchen's pocket. Beneath the glossy black ceiling a disco ball rotates lazily, sending light-blossoms—forget-me-nots, or bittersweet maybe—wheeling across the floor. The patterns warp, distort, as in a nightmare, when they hit the corners.

The stage is about the same height as the two beer crates stacked beside it. Facing the mirrored wall on stage, a girl coquettishly twirls her blond mane to the kind of pop music Jeanette likes. She's wearing nothing but a neon-green bikini bottom and struts back and forth on high heels. She throws a look at Dörchen, follows it with a longer, surprised one, and dances along the silken threads of that look. And when Dörchen sees that girl's face, something happens, though she can't quite say what, as if she's been startled by something familiar. Before she can figure it out, a slim brunette in a black trouser suit emerges from the string curtains around the bar alcove and approaches Dörchen.

'Good evening. What can I get you.'

What a voice. Dörchen orders a piccolo of Prosecco.

'Is anyone *else* joining you?'

Dörchen says no. Her heart is thumping again, at the base of her neck, on the left.

'Well then, enjoy yourself.'

Dörchen decides that anyone who makes it in here will get served one way or the other.

Two men are watching the girl on the stage. Sprawled in a seating area in front of the stage, they're being fawned over by two other half-naked girls. One of the guys had turned round when Dörchen was talking to the barmaid; now he says something to the other guy, and when the second guy and the girls turn round to look at Dörchen, the first gets up and comes over. 'Hello, love. Lost yer way?' He doesn't fit in here, really. White shirt, pressed trousers, respectable jacket, and the kind of glasses smart folk sometimes wear on TV. He grins, but Dörchen doesn't know what to say.

He clicks his fingers at the brunette, who's opening a piccolo in the bar alcove, and takes a seat on the banquette opposite Dörchen. 'Go on, tell us. What brings you to this place?' He's still grinning. Dörchen can tell a mean grin when she sees it; this one's just inquisitive. Besides, there's not much going on, not yet anyway. Maybe it doesn't really pick up until after midnight.

Okay, thinks Dörchen, here goes. 'I just wanted to see,' she says, 'what brought *Lothar* to this place.'

The brunette puts the piccolo bottle and a flute in front of Dörchen, and a brown drink with clinking ice in it in front of the man with the glasses. 'Lothar?' he says, 'Lothar who?'

Towards the end of the previous winter, Dörchen was woken up one night by Lothar's groaning. He had already been to the loo six or seven times, he said, but the urge to pee wasn't going away, just getting worse. The next morning he showed her a yellowish-brown bruise on the back of his hand. It looked like he'd hit it off something. But it was where he'd pressed his forehead against the back of his hand as he propped himself against the wall, trying to piss. Dörchen went with him to see the urologist. It was a nasty prostate infection, apparently. He had just about avoided being admitted to hospital and put on a drip there and then.

They'd sent him home with a prescription, and he had to put up with a catheter for a bit. 'That's definitely the end of it now. No more fishing,' said Dörchen, 'you'll catch your death yet.' But come spring he was up again at three in the morning and heading out—though his thingummy level never did go down—and it was nearly seven when he got home. He did that on an off all that time, got up at three and headed out, even after they'd had to take a biopsy. Once Dörchen heard him on the phone telling one of his friends from the club that he had 'eja… ejakillated blood, y'know what I mean?', and then a few weeks later he'd had the operation. Gitti, Günni and Dörchen were on the phone to each other several times a day.

It was while she was packing his case, when Lothar was transferring to the convalescent home in Bad Kissingen, that Dörchen found the matchbook in the pocket of his good jacket. Although she had occasionally wondered how come the jacket smelled of smoke—Lothar had given up smoking on New Year's Day 1978, after all—she hadn't made anything of it at first. And the matches could have been from that time he'd gone down the Reeperbahn after the company bash. All the same, following a hunch, Dörchen rang Horsti, the treasurer of the savings club, inventing some reason why she needed to know the balance in the account. When Horsti kept tying himself up in contradictory knots, she threatened to kick up a fuss sooner or later—at the very latest when they all gathered for the traditional *Grünkohl* dinner around Christmas.

'In five years we'll be celebrating our golden wedding anniversary,' Dörchen says to the man with the glasses, 'and God knows it wasn't all gold, but he gave up the drink thirty years ago, and this kind of thing,' she says, nodding at the room, 'he never did that anyway. I'd have noticed. He never did anything like that, and never needed to either.'

'He never did anything bad here, love,' says the man with the glasses. He knows which Lothar by now. He'd had his suspicions and called the blond girl over from the stage with a wave. 'He only ever drank mineral water, only flirted a bit, bought a girl the odd piccolo, offered a light, put on the charm and all that, but only ever with Chantal—right, Chantal?'

When she stood in front of them like that, the girl, one hip leaning against the balustrade, looking Dörchen openly in the eyes, Dörchen had that strange feeling again.

After an hour she makes to leave. '*How* much for one piccolo? Thirty-five euro? I'd get ten *big* bottles for that in Aldi!

The man grins. 'Better tell yer husband to go to Aldi next time so… '

'He can go to the devil, so he can,' mutters Dörchen.

The following afternoon, Sunday, instead of ringing Lothar first, as she would have other days, she phones Gitti to cancel. 'I've some class of a stomach bug,' she says, 'I can't even manage a cup of coffee, not to mind that carrot cake of yours.'

She spends the whole afternoon foostering in the kitchen, gives all the lamps in the living room a good going-over with the feather duster, beats the dust out of the corner sofa and cushions. In between she puts a Carl Bay record on the 10-stack record changer. Lothar had always resisted Günni and Gitti's attempts to make him sell off the old phonograph at the flea market, and Dörchen agreed with him; true, the kids had given Lothar a stereo for his birthday one time, but he'd never got the hang of 'them CDs'. She pulls another nine records out of their plastic-clad album covers—Caterina Valente, Peter Kraus, Bill Ramsey—and stacks them on the spindle, and it has grown dark outside by the time she pulls out the old photo albums as well, from the bottom drawer of the living-room cabinet, and begins to turn the pages in the light of the standard lamp, lifting the cardboard album cover with trembling fingers, and the fine protective paper between the pages of photos, and she's only on the third page when her heart starts pounding.

Beneath the black-and-white jagged-edged photo, in Dörchen's handwriting: 'In the Tivoli, 1958.' What a fine figure of a man he was; how her stomach used to flutter when she ran her fingers through his quiff; and those stylish cufflinks… And then she looks at herself; she remembers being caught off guard by Ewald— poor Ewald who departed this world in 1966—and now, seeing her own face of 1958 looking back at her, her heart starts pounding in her neck. As usual when she needs to calm down—especially since she's got older—she has the urge to speak out loud. 'Only the hair's different,' she murmurs, as she looks at her face, 'but apart from that…' The lips, nose, forehead and eyes, the fresh, innocent expression on the face—'Just like that Chantal girl,' Dörchen murmurs. 'Just like that Chantal.'

She's still sitting in Lothar's wing chair when the cuckoo clock strikes twelve; she never did phone Lothar, and when the phone rang, she didn't answer it. For hours she has been thinking of the yellowish-brown bruise on the back of Lothar's hand, where he leaned his forehead night after night, standing over the toilet, seat up, trying to squeeze out a few drops; and Lothar's hands had been exposed all sorts of things in his lifetime, bricks and mortar, wind and weather, hammer-blows and the devil knows what, for all of forty years.

At some point Dörchen falls asleep in the armchair; next morning she phones Gitti and asks her to buy her a ticket for the train to Bad Kissingen, 'just a single for now; I'll do the return bit with Papa.' Suddenly, from the minute she'd woken up, there was nothing she wanted more than to see in the winter with Lothar.

Depiction

To form eyes she cut two holes
in the paper,
neither round nor oval
more like buttonholes
stretched out of shape.
He wasn't a real liar, she explained,
but ugliness attracted her, coarse hands
thick voices, scarred and burnt skin.
Only this, she said, could do justice
to his hefty stare.
His face was cocked to one side
slightly, as if inviting a blow,
the ears she had drawn
seemed to be climbing towards
the top of the head.
She had scribbled him some hair,
briskly rubbed dark paint into the cheeks
to show his stubble,
like a boy wiping away an unwanted kiss.
The lines of the nose ran parallel
before swerving round
to meet each other.
She tore the mouth open
with her fingers, folded back
the helpless lips,
then wrote words below the face,
stacks of words he had forced to rhyme,
numb words she swore she had heard him say,
words he could never take back.

Gavan Duffy

Bottles
Michael Nolan

It started in Boots. We were in for false tan, or lipstick. Eyeliner maybe. Karen was down on her hunkers looking through face creams on the bottom shelf. I was standing with my hands in my pockets, trying not to let the brightness of white lights get to me. I walked to the end of the aisle, passed an auld doll with a basket full of cotton pads, and stopped at the men's section. Electronic razors, beard trimmers, aftershave balm and all the bollocks of the day.

I went to the next aisle, the Durex section. Purple and pink bottles. Tingle. Massage Oil. Enhanced Lubrication. A lesser man would shy away. Not me. I'd the vibrating ring in my hand trying to work out the point of it. Then the lubrication oil, gel that tastes like blueberries, numbing gel for those who can't last the duration of opening credits.

Karen appeared at my shoulder like a bad feeling. 'What're ye doin?'

'Just havin a look.'

She spotted discount nail polish on the opposite shelf. Bold orange, almost luminous. She checked the colour on the miniscule brush, glanced round and took a stealthy whiff.

'Pregnancy tests,' I said, pointing.

'What do you want with them?'

I lifted one that told you the result and how many weeks along. 'Do they work? Like, are they accurate?'

'Seriously, how would I know?'

'Have you never done one?'

She gave me a filthy look, set the nail polish back and walked away.

I read the box. There were no instructions, only facts about its accuracy and how easy it was to use. Not just a piss-stick anymore, this was state-of-the-art technology. Innovative, like those at-home STI tests I'd seen advertised. I held it up to read the small print. A group of teenage girls reeking of tester-bottle perfume spotted me and laughed.

'It's not for me,' I said, and they looked at me like I should be taken home.

I met Karen at the till. She was hugging a bundle of tan and hair products to her chest and texting with her one free hand. Her face was taut with impatience, hair tied back in a bun, and the more I stared at her the more determined she seemed to text on her phone. 'I reckon you should do one,' I said. 'Just for the craic.'

'Go away.'

'Why not? It would be good to see how it works.'

'You piss on it and it tells you if you're pregnant. That's it.'

The woman at the till stared, pencilled eyebrows giving her the look of being in a state of perpetual shock.

'It's mad though, isn't it? Tells ye how many weeks and all. It would be good to do it for the craic I reckon, wouldn't it?'

She locked her phone screen and dropped it into the depths of her handbag, and the woman took her things and scanned them with a flourish and a beep.

I was working nightshift in the Coca-Cola factory, so we didn't get much time together. Going to Boots and knocking about town was the height of it. In Starbucks, we ordered gingerbread lattes because it was Christmas. The place was packed with the hum of conversation and cosiness of heat. Lads and girls with scarves to their knees sat perched over giant mugs blowing into froth.

We got a table upstairs by the windows overlooking Arthur's Square, the Spirit of Belfast sculpture that looked more like giant intertwined onion rings than anything else. Groups of groomed nightclub PRs with tight haircuts and handfuls of flyers sat about the base. Teenagers congregated and broke apart, smoked fegs and kissed. Karen had her phone out again, fingers blitzing across the screen. She sipped her drink and continued texting with her free hand, glancing at me then across the room like I should have something better to do than watch her.

'Do you wash the piss off after you get the result?' I said.

She didn't take her eyes from her phone.

'Like, when you do a pregnancy test and it comes out positive, do you wash the piss away?'

'You're a weirdo.'

'Do you ever see in films and TV though? When they see they're pregnant they run about wavin it in the air. People grab it to see for themselves, but there's piss all over it. Some girl has pissed all over it and every cunt's grabbin it.'

'Seriously. You need to stop.'

She went back to her phone all flustered and swiped her thumb down the screen. Onto Facebook now, scrolling through her Newsfeed, staring at selfies of people she doesn't even like.

I looked out the window. There was a busker at the top of Anne's Street. Ginger hair, brown shoes and a big coat. Beard as patchy as his singing, his eyes closed and rolled back when he went for the high notes. Another Rupert Grint looking cunt singing Ed Sheeran songs. A group of lads stopped in front of him and sang along. One went to grab his empty guitar case, his precious hard earned shrapnel, and jumped back laughing from his angry kick.

'Imagine you did one and it came out positive,' I said.

She couldn't even look at me.

She worked in a clothes shop. She got the job through the Steps to Work programme with the Job Centre. They put her there, and for six months she'd to do full-time hours for an extra fifteen on her dole. Serving customers, arranging clothes on hangers, standing outside changing rooms for hours at a time with no one to talk to but herself. She hated it, dreaded it even when she was taken on and paid full wages.

I spent most nights on the settee. She couldn't put up with me coming home at six in the morning and waking her. So I'd come in quietly, close the door slow, always careful to tiptoe my way down the hall and into the living room. I wouldn't turn the TV on, didn't even have the balls to flush the toilet if I'd to piss. She needed her sleep for the clothes shop. She was better with her sleep.

That morning, I came home from work and heard music even before I opened the front door. Stifled voices and laughter. I stepped into the hall and saw the light on below the bedroom door. There was a delighted scream, bed sheets rustling, creaking of bed-frame and floorboards. Karen was naked. Someone was with her and they were laughing at me, rolling about the bed laughing with each other, singing along to songs they didn't know the words to and shrieking with glee.

I stood in the hall, the sounds of unhindered voices bashing through me. She was never usually home at this time. She'd go to house parties or illegal raves, anything to prolong the night. I wouldn't usually see her until the next afternoon. I leant against the wall to steady myself, took a breath and tried to swallow, my chest tightening from excitement or fear, I wasn't sure, only collapsing.

She opened the door before I could. She was in a dress, her hair curled and eyelashes black with mascara. She jumped back when she saw me, then looked disappointed I wasn't somebody else.

'We went out,' she said. 'Shona needed to get out. She's not having a good time of it. She's staying with us and needed a girly night so we went out for a girly night.'

Her friend Shona was spread-eagled on the bed staring up at the ceiling. Her skirt rode up her thighs, big chest lumping out and rolling back to her chin like an extra stomach. 'I need water,' she said. 'I need water and food. And socks. My feet are freezin. Get me socks.'

Karen turned to me. 'Is there something you want?'

She raised her eyebrows, glazed eyes stubborn with exasperation. She liked to speak properly after a few drinks, liked to fool herself into believing good annunciation was who she was.

Shona sat up and pointed. 'Look at his high-vis,' she said. 'Ach bless.' She went into hysterics and rolled across the bed. 'You look like a wee workin man. And the boots. Oh Mummy. Are they steel toe-capped? Karen, he's actually wearin steel toe-caps.'

Karen nearly keeled over. She'd to grab hold of the door handle and cradle her stomach she laughed so hard.

I left them to it and went into the living room. It was open planned, the kitchen a mess of unwashed glasses and food-stained plates, the breakfast bar all burnt-out candles and wet tea towels. There was a blanket and one pillow waiting for me on the settee. I took my boots and jacket off, lay down and curled up into a ball.

I could see myself reflected in the blank TV screen. A dull figure. Orange gauze of streetlight broke between half-open blinds. I tried not to hear what they were saying in the bedroom but their voices carried. Something about a party and dancing with someone. That creepy fella with the tattoo. I closed my eyes to sleep and the music faded. I heard something about the toilets and more cackles of laughter. Someone's arse.

I thought of where I'd go if I walked out. There was something appealing about the idea of a bench, of lying flat and staring at the sky while the deadness of the city ached around me. I thought of all the things that could happen to me, the coldness chewing through toes and fingers, people shouting for taxis home from nightclubs and starting punch-ups outside the twenty-four hour McDonalds. I pictured myself being trailed from my bench and kicked in the face and heard the laughter in the next room.

They whaled into the kitchen at one point, shushing each other and whispering. I kept my eyes closed and held my stillness. But it didn't stop them opening and slamming cupboards, rummaging through drawers, ripping open packets of crisps, chewing and smacking and blasting water taps.

'Ye shouldn't be drinkin in your state,' Shona said. 'Twenty-four weeks along. Ye can't be steamin at twenty-four weeks.'

'Sure if I can't do it now, when can I ever?'

I looked up and they both went into a fit of laughter. Karen had a pillow stuffed up her dress and was cradling it in her arms. 'Is this what you want?' she said. 'Our wee baby.'

'Sorry,' Shona said. 'It's mine. We've been havin an affair.'

'These things happen …'

'The pregnancy test. Show him the pregnancy test.'

'Can't. There's piss all over it.'

I was out the door before either of them got up. The sun was low in the sky and blinding—like its good night's sleep was something to scream about. The pavement white with ice and grit. Black taxis charged round the depot across the street, drivers shouted between windows and heavy doors opened and slammed. A group of lads in tracksuits came out of a shop drinking bottles of energy drink. I could feel the soreness in my feet. I wasn't angry. I wasn't even fed-up. I was tired and I was walking. The cold air did me a world of good and I felt a wistful despondency at being hard done by. It made me content to be alone, going somewhere and doing something, even if it was just walking.

Girls in body warmers and Ugg boots pushed prams between charity shops. I passed a group of drunks sitting on the pavement with their backs against the wall, bleating like lambs. A woman in white leggings sat between them. She squinted at me, licked her chapped lips and grinned. Tourists with cameras round their necks stared about like they weren't sure this was the right place.

Nobody I knew was about, not even Maxi. He loved Castle Street, loved the drunks and the ruffians, the lads knocking out weed and stolen perfume on side streets. Last time I saw him he was marching up and down the pavement with a takeout cup asking people for change. I gave him two quid and he called me a miserable bastard. He wasn't even homeless. His head was in the shed but he wasn't homeless.

Roma women with *Big Issues* tried to make a sale. Men in suits strutted between coffee shops and bank buildings, coat-tails whipping out like twenty-first century barons of online banking. I walked in circles and laps, passed McDonalds at the corner of Castle Place three times, the same whiff of deep fat fryers and microwaved processed meat wafting through me again and again. I glanced at the green copper coated domes of the City Hall and passed nightclub PRs like I had somewhere to go.

They were probably awake now. Shona was probably unpacking her clothes while Karen made space for her. New toothbrush in the cup by the sink, pyjamas and knickers folded and stuffed into drawers, her phone taking its place on my bedside table. I dreaded the thought of going back, hoped only that they'd clean the place, that I could at least fill myself a glass of water without stressing about it tasting of vodka.

I went to Boots on Royal Avenue and stared at pregnancy tests. Women passed me and looked at me like I might steal their handbags. Others went to self-checkouts and scanned items uncertainly. I left and went back again. Employees in white tunics began to recognise me. They patrolled aisles like screws and I left and went to the branch in Castle Court, lifted one of the tests and read the box. I couldn't buy it. I got as far as the till, the woman blinking at me, before I dropped it on the floor and ran.

I ended up sitting at the base of the Spirit of Belfast sculpture. The town milled around me. People crossed and re-crossed Arthur's Square like bottles on a conveyor belt. There were no buskers and it was too early yet for the usual clusters of teenagers. Some people sat at tables by the windows of Starbucks hunched over coffees, watching. I half expected something to happen, someone to slap me on the back of the head or step on my foot.

I tried to think of how it might work with Shona. I would come in from my night-shift and sleep on the settee. Karen would get up in the morning and go to work and Shona would … what? She was unemployed, signing on, and I felt for her because I knew what it was like. But she was sleeping on my side of the bed. She was drooling on my pillow and showering in my en-suite bathroom. She was eating the crisps I had stashed in the cupboard below the sink and leaving takeout cartons at her arse. I pictured us alone in the apartment while Karen was at work. Shona taking over the settee, flicking through channels on the TV, and me on the floor or at the breakfast bar trying to think of things to say and saying them all wrong. I'd have to get out. I'd have to walk about town and see things I see too much of and pretend they don't break my heart each time I see them.

Castle Street. McDonalds. The copper green domes of the City Hall.

I couldn't face it and yet I had to. I already was. I was sitting in Arthur Square with nowhere to go, and the only thing I could think of doing I couldn't bring myself to do. No bother lifting a vibrating ring or lubricant or flavoured gels. I wouldn't break a sweat bringing any of them to the counter. But a pregnancy test?

There was something so definitive about a result. An absolute yes or no. I knew which of these categories I fell into but I wanted to see. I didn't care how it worked. Like a diabetes test or a thermometer, it just did. The stick reacted to your piss, the display showed you a result, there was nothing else to it, yet there was everything, and I wanted to witness everything. My result. Then I would be something. I would have something to hold up and say this is me, this is what I am.

A baby dropped its dodo on the ground and a man bent down to pick it up.

There are two places in town you're likely to find Maxi. Outside Smithfield at the back of Castle Court, or round by St Anne's Cathedral with a dip of glue unable to tell his arse from his elbow. So Smithfield it was. He was standing with his back against the wall of the carpet shop. He'd his hood up. Thirty years old and he's walking about town in tracksuit bottoms and his hood up. Pale and skinny as a feg, he'd the look of someone unused to daylight. 'What's happenin, cunt ye?'

He spoke with a squeal, forcing words out of himself as if fingers were gently and relentlessly pressing on his throat. And his smile was massive, his eyes wild and glassy. Movements and reactions always exaggerated. When a woman passed in skinny jeans he craned his neck, stared wide-eyed at her arse and threw his hands in the air like he'd never seen anything like it.

'This town's teemin with it,' he said. 'They're everywhere. Big buck me boots and all. I love it. I seriously fuckin love it. Didn't dress like that when we were growin up, did they?'

'Tracksuits and guddies. Pyjama bottoms on a good day.'

He agreed and laughed, delighted. He skipped on the spot and rubbed his hands together, veins like pathways on his arms, then leaned back against the wall. 'What is it you're lookin?' he said. 'I know you're not here for nothin. You're lookin somethin. I can tell by your eyes. What is it? Tell me and I'll get ye anything ye want.'

I don't know how I know him. We might have been from the same place or went to the same school, but I can't picture or remember him being anything other than how he is now. Not as a boy or a teenager or in a school uniform. He was always Maxi who loved a dip of glue. Maxi with the clammy sore skin, the battered face and skeletal frame too skeletal for the smallest sized clothes. They hung on him like a bad life, hunching him over, bottoms of his tracksuit bottoms dragging across the ground gathering dirt, tearing.

'I need you to do somethin for me,' I told him. 'I'll pay ye.'

He buried his hands in his pockets and looked up and down the street. 'Go ahead will,' he said. 'What do ye need? Tell me. Go on. Wait. Hold on.'

An aul fella came out of the carpet shop and draped a maroon floor mat over the railings beside us. He stepped back to see it better, scratched the back of his head and pulled his trousers up. He saw us and nodded, spat on the ground and went back inside. 'Go on,' Maxi said. 'What do ye need?'

'I need ye to get me somethin in Castle Court.'

'Much you payin?'

'Plenty.'

He narrowed his eyes, stepped forward as if to see me better. 'You up to somethin? You're a hairy bear. I know you're up to no good. I fuckin love it.'

'You'll do it then?'

He threw his head back and howled like a man possessed. 'Mon the fuck. I'll do anything.'

He skipped on the spot and we crossed the road to Castle Court. People queued at the bank machine and Maxi stayed a step behind, glancing left and right as we went through the shopping centre doors. 'It's not Debenhams, is it?' he said. 'I can't go near Debenhams. Got scooped strokin nail polish a few weeks ago. Can't go near it.'

Inside, he glanced up at the ceiling for cameras, then at the passing faces of people like they were undercover, and ducked his head. A baby was crying, its whimpers echoing in the expanse. Footsteps clicked and clacked on the floors. Music blared out of Burton and Miss Selfridge and JD Sports and I saw a woman sit on a bench, take a shoe off and rub her foot. A man was sitting next to her eating cereal straight out of the box and staring round. Every shop seemed to have a sale on, big red posters like stop signs in the din.

We stopped outside Boots. I handed him two score notes and told him what I wanted. 'Keep the twenty for yourself,' I said. 'And keep the change from that twenty. Just make sure it's that exact model, right?'

He frowned at the cash, looked me dead in the face but didn't ask what the test was for.

'Do you hear me? The one that says how many weeks. Make sure it's that one.'

He looked into Boots, at the women with veneered teeth and blusher-peppered faces, and I could see the hesitance in his eyes. 'Right,' he said, and took a step forward and stopped. He took the two twenty quid notes and held them up to the light, squinting, checking and making sure.

'I know what you're like, ballbag. You'd stroke the laces from my guddies right and quick.'

They were still there when I got back to the apartment that afternoon. At the breakfast bar with a half-eaten takeout between them, a bottle of wine and two glasses. They looked at me, then at Maxi like he should have a wash before stepping closer.

'We're having a drink,' Karen said. Her face was pale and craggy like scuffed paper. Traces of runny mascara on her cheeks. Shona chewed the skin round the nail of her thumb. She was wearing a pair of Karen's pyjama shorts, big legs streaked with false tan.

I sat on the settee and Maxi looked between them, his posture shrinking back, folding into himself. He'd a bag full of bottles of nail polish he'd bought with the money I gave him. He held it to his chest and sat on the edge of the settee next to me. He sniffed, and swallowed a lug of phlegm. He put me in mind of a foster child and I wondered if he ever was one.

'Do you wanna watch TV?' I asked him, and he shook his head.

'I wanna drink, or a toke of somethin.'

'We've wine here,' Karen said. 'Mon over and have a glass.'

He got up and approached them reluctantly, kept his eyes on their faces as a cup was filled and handed to him.

'Sit down sure,' Shona said. 'What's your name? Maxi? Sit you down and talk to us, Maxi.'

Maxi rubbed his hand on his thigh, clutched his bag of nail polish to him.

'Who's the nail polish for? Can we see them?'

'No. They're for my girl.'

'What's her name?'

He shrugged and raised the cup to his lips, took a large gulp and grimaced. Karen and Shona laughed, asked him did he not like it. 'I do,' he said. 'I'd drink anything.'

They asked him where he was from, how he knew me and if he wanted some chips. 'They've been there a few hours,' said Shona. 'But sure they'll be sweet.'

Maxi nodded and frowned at the floor, his eyes distrustful. He coughed into his hand and swallowed. Karen struggled to hide her disgust. 'So what do you do with yourself? Are you working anywhere?'

I left them to it and went into the bedroom. There was an open suitcase filled with clothes on the bed. The iron had been left on the floor and had burnt the edge of the bed sheet it was leant against. I flicked the switch off, went into the en-suite bathroom, locked the door and sat down.

I could hear them in the living room. They continued speaking like I wasn't listening. Karen asked Maxi what he was doing with me. 'I hope you're not getting him into trouble,' she said. 'Are you?'

I almost heard his shoulders shrug. 'We had to do somethin.'

I stared around the bathroom. The lime green floor mat was dishevelled. It matched the lime green tiles and the lime great soap dispenser and the lime green toilet roll holder. The white and lime green shower curtain was half closed and the lime green shower mat had become unstuck from the bathtub. I took the pregnancy test from my back pocket and made sure the door was locked.

Clear Blue. Ninety-seven percent accurate. Longer ergonomic shape makes it easier to handle and more hygienic—less likely to piss on your hand—and you can test up to four days before your period's due. Unmistakably clear digital results within three minutes …

Three minutes. Longer time waiting on the result than it takes to piss.

There was a scream in the living room. Something dropped and smashed. Silence, then an eruption of laughter. Maxi was getting more animated. I heard his voice raised and I heard Shona say something about him being far better craic than I was.

I opened the box and took out the test. It looked like an electronic thermometer. Sleek and white with a fat blue tip and little square screen. I held it up to the light and wondered how many people had used it and got the result they didn't want. The bad news breaker. An almost immediate, three-minute diagnosis at a tenner a go.

What do they do for three minutes? Where do their minds go? A torturous life-changing wait. Karen wouldn't have it. Thirty seconds was about as long as she was willing to wait for anything.

The door knocked and I froze.

'You in there?'

It was her. The handle went down and there was a push.

'What're you doing? I need to speak to you.'

I stuffed the stick in my pocket, dumped the box at the bottom of the lime green bin by the sink and let her in.

'I was takin a piss,' I said. 'Is that all right?'

'I didn't hear the toilet flush.'

She stepped round me and checked the bowl. I reached passed her and flushed it. 'What's the matter?'

She sighed, put the lid down and sat. She squeezed her hands between her thighs, tensed her shoulders like she was cold and looked up at me. She looked small and stranded, eyes glassy with drink and lack of sleep. She liked a drink, liked partying, but not bringing the party home. Her home was where she came back to, where she'd wash her makeup off and put her pyjamas on. She liked lying on the settee and watching box-sets all day, eating chocolate and junk food and cradling her hangover to her. That was her favourite part, the binge-eating recovery before going back to work, and I could tell she missed it, that she was afraid of the next day.

'Shona has nowhere to go,' she said. 'What am I gonna do?'

Maxi's voice was loud now. Something about running away from someone. Peelers probably. Shona was lapping it up, her exaggerated laughter as irritating as her voice. Karen groaned and sighed again. 'What am I gonna do?'

I'd my hand in my pocket and could feel the plastic stick between my fingers. 'I just can't,' she said. 'I'm dyin a death. This is too much and I dunno how long she'll be staying. I can't …'

Her words ran into each other and off into nothing, and I knelt down in front of her. Her bare knees were cold. Goose pimples exploded along her thighs. She was shivering and staring into space with gloom.

'Throw them out and blame it on me.'

The words tumbled from my mouth before I could stop myself, and she sat up and grinned with relief. She hugged me and I hugged her back with one hand still in my pocket. Then, like she realised what she was doing, she pushed me away, stood up, and checked herself in the mirror with a renewed resolve.

'You can stay in here if you want, or come out with me. I don't care.'

'I'll stay here sure,' I said. 'Go you on.'

She was about to retort, but stopped herself and took a breath. Her hands were shaking and for a moment I wanted to grab hold of her fingers, steady her.

I listened to her call me all the names of the day and tell them they had to go. I sat on the toilet and waited. 'He won't have it,' she said. 'He wants you out. There's nothing I can do ...'

She whimpered and shrieked and I kept the pregnancy test in my pocket. It poked into my upper thigh like a blunt pencil. Shona tried to reassure her. She understood. She'd find somewhere else to go. 'Don't worry about me,' she said. 'I'll be sweet. Don't worry yourself.'

A door slammed. Maxi walking out probably. I took the test from my pocket again and held it out. Clear Blue as day. Plus for positive, minus for negative. Negative for nothing.

I stood, unbuttoned my jeans and changed my mind, sat down. If I was going to do this I was going to do it right.

I pressed my hand on myself so I'd piss downwards into the bowl, leant forward and reached round as if to wipe my arse and held the stick under. My hand was trembling, thighs straining mid-squat. I could have fallen forward but I didn't. I held.

Shona was on the phone to someone and Karen apologised again and again. 'It's him. It's all his fault. I hate him. I wish he'd go ...'

I stared at the tiled floor. There was a red stain by the radiator that looked like blood. A single blob. I could see the minute dots of splash round the outer circle. Perfectly red and round like someone had done it intentionally. They had squeezed the cut on their finger and held it out, waited, holding themselves as the blood gathered and throbbed, suspended, forming into a drip as they squeezed harder still, persuading it to fall. And it did fall. It fell and hit the tile, and the silence with which it hit was unbroken, like the blood had issued from the tile itself and stayed there, waiting to be wiped.

I held the test out and, careful not to let it drip, gave it a shake and pointed the tip downwards. The instructions said to keep it held down or to set it on a flat surface and wait three minutes.

I pictured Karen sitting on the toilet not long before, her spoiled look of haplessness, the things she said and the way she said them, and I felt, for the first time in a long time, the sweeping sensation of knowing exactly what I wanted and had to do. It was sudden and uplifting and I stood and pulled my jeans up, didn't bother washing the piss from my hands or the wetness from the stick. My purpose was my time and I had to fulfil it or break down.

She was back at the breakfast bar dabbing her eyes with kitchen roll, the same desolate look on her face. The cowering of herself, of her being terribly wronged.

Shona was texting on her phone. She looked at me apologetically, like someone suddenly realising they've done wrong.

'I'll be out of your hair,' she said. 'I don't wanna be a problem. I don't wanna impose. I'm so sorry …'

'You're not imposing,' Karen said. 'You're not doing anything wrong. It's him.'

Her contempt was unconvincing, and I held my hands out. 'I'm sorry,' I said. 'I didn't mean to react badly.'

I went to Shona and placed a wet hand on her shoulder. She looked at it, then at my face. I sighed heavily and shook my head. 'This was all just a bit sudden for me. I didn't mean to react as I did. Please,' I said, and I squeezed her shoulder. 'Please stay with us. I want you to stay with us. It's the least we can do with all you're goin through.'

She turned to Karen whose mouth fell open, her look of panic lingering for a tenth of a second too long. 'Are ye sure?' she said. 'Like, I'll find somewhere else. Maxi offered me his settee …'

'You can't stay with Maxi. You're stayin with us.'

'Are you sure?'

'Of course, Shona. You're welcome here for as long as you need.'

She was stunned, and when she glanced at Karen I knew part of her regretted treating me as she had.

'Thank you so much.' Her chin wobbled, that heart-swelling sensation of having someone care seeping through her. 'I should tell Maxi,' she said.

'Is he not away?'

'No. He's in the blue bathroom.'

She took another breath to compose herself and left the room with her phone in hand. Karen went to follow, then stopped halfway. She looked at me like I would regret this, like this was the final straw, and I didn't care. I smiled and shrugged like it was the least I could do.

How many minutes had gone by? Couldn't be three. Not yet.

'I'll stay on the settee sure,' I said. 'Yous can have the bed, I don't mind.'

Before she could say anything, Shona screamed. Something dropped to the floor with a clink. Karen and I looked at each other, distrusting ourselves, distrusting the yelp, and scampered out to the hall to the blue bathroom.

Shona had the door open, one hand on the handle, reeling. 'What's he doin?' she said. 'What the fuck?'

Maxi was standing by the sink, a litter of empty nail polish bottles scattered at his feet. He'd his plastic bag held to his mouth, the inside all splattered blue, pink and bright orange, and he was sucking from it, deep long intakes of air as he swayed. His eyes were half closed and he gazed at us as if from across a road, a mile-wide road, and he waved and smiled and sucked deeper, the bag crumpling and crackling like static on a badly tuned TV.

The smell was overwhelming. Karen covered her mouth and nose. Shona watched with wide eyes. She giggled, glanced between us and him and stepped back. Maxi raised a hand, took a deep inhalation and let it drop. He closed his eyes and stumbled against the sink, then slowly raised his chin up and up until he stared at the ceiling. A silent moment of suspended high. I could almost see him lifting, rising up with his expanding lungs and—just as I thought he was about to go, right as his tip toes were about to leave the floor and drift upwards—there was a beep. Two beeps. Beep Beep.

Karen and Shona looked at me. 'What was that?'

I took the pregnancy test from my pocket and held it out. Maxi's bag crackled and he exhaled.

Negative.

Jessica

We glued
her head by
the right cheek to
the mirror
she had loved so much, had
gazed so fondly into, fascinated
by the mirror-face that showed her
new expressions. After much discussion (we didn't want
to blow it) we inserted
ten acutes of
thin glass triangles
into her blue eyes, so they
fanned from the sockets
like rays. She
had pages
on social networks, with photos of herself
and a boxer
called Joe. Joe's
dead now, of course
in the hall, beside
the rest
of her. They go everywhere
together, Joe and Jessica. For a while
there was a little
white cloud, or halo
on the glass, where her warmth
rested. We stood and watched, as
slowly, it
departed.

Roderick Ford

Milf

The dead
are making babies still
fucking in porno clips
on the web. That's my mummy
opening her legs
for that hairy
man. Was I conceived just then, is that bearded
bloke my da, who hugs her
close and gentle in the year
that she was beaten for
an hour, and died in the back room
of The Angel's Head?
                    I watch her
do it all again—I'm sure
she likes him, her smile's so real, so's
the way she comes. Does
she sense we're all around, unseen
and watching
over her, and maybe even guess
I'm out here too, staring
at the pearly gates
that I came through?
                    Before
I'm older than her twenty nine
I want to do a film of Jimmy
fucking me, and leave
it near her in the web's forever now. You'll find us
listed under deep-down milfs, perhaps
with offspring still to come, all fruit
upon an endless vine.
                    But I'm glad
I can download my mum, know
the fierce embraces
that she gives, proud to have her here
in my own room, the way
she once welcomed me
into her salty womb, and kept me safe, a mad life
bouncing in its padded cell, while her red
heart roared up above, and broke
like the arms of the sea.

Roderick Ford

Tales of our Time
Cathy Sweeney

[1] The Cheerleader

The cheerleader had a God-given talent for cheerleading. On days when the wind cracked stones she smothered herself in Vaseline and cheered on the cold. Boy could that girl cheer. She cheered in nursing homes and funeral parlours and empty football stadiums, sucking up negative ions like sweets and handing out smiles like candy. Every morning she ate cheer for breakfast. When bits of her began breaking she worried that people would notice but they never did. What matter a stump for a leg or a wire hanger where an arm should be? Red skirt + white socks + pom-poms = cheerleader.

[2] The Show Trial

I went to see the show trial because someone said it would be fun. They said it would be fun because no one ever knew what the show trial was showing and only rarely could you figure out who was guilty and who was innocent. It was against my sense of identity to attend such an entertainment but I went anyway. At the booth I haggled with the girl until she gave me a discount on a return ticket to the end of the night. The girl came out of the booth carrying a small flash lamp and led me to an opening in a large blue tent. She wore knee high white boots that made a sound like a kiss when she walked and I was glad I had come. Inside the tent words from the microphone threw shadows on the red walls and I had to stoop to find a seat. A woman was on trial. She was extremely fat and people around me laughed inconsolably. In the tradition of the court procedures the woman wore only her underwear. She was delighted with the attention. People spoke to her and called her by her name and touched her to show that they were not afraid of her. Their words echoed through the microphone and lengthened darkly on the red walls. The woman was found guilty on two counts of poverty—

real and imagined—and taken reluctantly from the dock. There were many other show trials that night but you know how it is, a man only remembers his first.

[3] Orwell's Nose

George Orwell had a very large nose. It jutted out from between his eyes like a gigantic keel, making his eyes appear small. When he changed his name from Eric Blair, Orwell secretly hoped that his nose might change too but, if anything, it grew larger. At the outbreak of World War Two, Orwell was declared unfit for military service on account of his nose. So humungous was it that it had developed the ability to smell normally odourless gases. As you might expect, Orwell felt it his duty to report his findings, both to those in positions of power as well as to ordinary people in the street. This was a mistake. There are some gases that nobody wants to know about, especially in times of war. Orwell continued smelling anyway. With a nose like that he had no choice. Of course, you won't see an incredibly large nose in any photographs of George Orwell. They were airbrushed out years ago. We need to be able to love our heroes.

[4] A Love Story

There once was a woman who loved her husband's cock so much that she began taking it to work in her lunchbox. It was early in the marriage and the husband had not yet decided what his wife could have and what she could not—they were still in love—and so he went along with her little peccadillo. In the mornings, after the man had showered, the wife would take the cock and wrap it in cling film and put it in her lunchbox alongside her bratwurst sandwich, portion of fruit, and chocolate biscuit—everyone needs a treat! In the evenings when she returned from work the wife would matter-of-factly return the cock to her husband before preparing their evening meal—venison stew or beef casserole or sometimes the husband's favourite, the French dish called chicken-in-wine. It was no doubt an unusual arrangement but right up until the husband filed for divorce it seemed to suit both parties. Of course, the divorce lawyers went to town about a cock in a lunchbox and there was some unsavoury press coverage. When it was all over the wife got a new job in a new town and took up pottery. She became very good at it and exhibitions of her work were held biannually. The husband married the woman he had fallen in love with. She was young and modern and had no need of his or anyone else's cock, thank you very much. The funny thing was that years later, when the husband occasionally put his hand to his crotch and found his cock firmly in place, he experienced an intense but short-lived nostalgia for the good old days.

[5] History Project: Topic—The Great Crisis

The first case was that of a young boy in Venezuela. Santiago Enrique Pedroza, then aged fourteen, was out gathering firewood with his sister and a friend when he disappeared. As his sister later recounted, Santiago walked ahead of her and the friend and had just crossed a little stream beside a wild rose bush when he appeared to lose his balance and 'fall' off the surface of the earth. The story soon faded from the press. People said the children were on drugs and anyway, quite a lot of people disappear in Venezuela. The second case was not so easy to dismiss. Inga Steinhaus was a woman in her fifties who lived in the suburbs of Frankfurt with her husband and three sons. She was walking home from the bakery one day along a busy street when, according to witnesses, she appeared to stumble and 'fall' off the earth. Her screams could be heard for a full minute. One witness managed to take a photograph before Frau Steinhaus disappeared from view. The image shows a middle-aged woman 'falling' upwards into the sky, her mouth agape, her trench coat flapping around her. The loaf of bread and bag of pastries that she had bought in the bakery were found at the scene. They had dropped from her basket as she 'fell', as did her keys which, it was deduced, slipped from her pocket. The media reported the Frau Steinhaus story and within twenty-four hours the photograph of her 'falling' became the most viewed photograph in history. There were many conspiracy theories—that Frau Steinhaus was a computerised blow up doll, that NASA had developed a VACWEP [vacuum weapon] that malfunctioned, that aliens had become more brazen in their abductions—but the grief of the family seemed real. And that was that for over a year. I wouldn't say Frau Steinhaus was forgotten—a band called themselves after her and she had an entry on Wikipedia—but the story faded. The third case was that of Nancy Millar from New York State who was out bicycling with her boyfriend one Sunday afternoon. The boyfriend heard the crash of a bicycle behind him and turned around to find Nancy had disappeared. Looking upwards he glimpsed something red in the blue sky and later confirmed that Nancy had been wearing red shorts. The media covered the story in great detail and a cross nation expert scientific committee called CNESC was set up to investigate the three incidents. No sooner had they met but all hell broke loose. People began 'falling' off the earth in droves. In the following days, 'incidents'—as they were called—were reported in Scotland, Alaska, Nebraska, The Netherlands, Fiji and Paris. 'Incidents' were reported during the night as well as during the day. As its homepage, Google created an interactive map of the world with red dots where 'incidents' occurred. Soon there were red dots everywhere and Google was ordered to take down the map. It put up a picture of white flowers instead. For a while people stopped going out unless they were poor and had to, or they went out in armoured cars. Companies who got in early on 'incident-proof-products' made a fortune. Lead boots were particularly popular. CNESC worked around the clock to find an explanation for the 'incidents' but could not find one. Religious mania increased, as did nihilism. And then the 'incidents' stopped. Days passed, and then months, and then a year, with no reports of anyone 'falling' off the surface of the earth. Gradually things got back to normal. During the Great Crisis—as it came to be called—the death count from starvation, illness, violence and suicide far exceeded the total number of 'incidents' but no one talked about that. In fact, soon no one talked much about the 'incidents'. That is all.

[6] Another Love Story

This story happened twenty years ago when the world was very different from today. For one thing, morals were looser and people engaged in acts of depravity without so much as a by-your-leave. And for another thing, everyone was ignorant and believed in strange happenings beyond the here and now. I tell you this so that you will have some sympathy for the main character of this story—a farmer —and not judge him according to the good and high sensibilities of our time, but cut him some slack on account of the backward age he was born into. The farmer was a young man—he was in his prime—but, on account of the depopulation of the countryside, he had no wife. So, after a long hot summer of ploughing furrows and stemming dykes and planting rods, he came up to the city with a handful of cash and a hard cock. The farmer, as I am sure you can understand, was looking for some action and, after conferring with the hotel concierge, a small man with a large moustache and a knowledge of the ways of the world, the farmer—showered, shaved and togged out in a new shirt—headed off in the direction of the cabaret. There he found, as you can imagine, an establishment exactly congruous to his needs. With its velvet curtains and dark furniture, the cabaret was perfectly aligned with Eros and straightaway the farmer found himself in a red booth choosing hungrily from a menu that came with a free cocktail. Handing over his handful of cash to a smiling madame, he went straight for the complete works—**Full Body incl. Head**—and had, as soon as his order arrived, as again I'm sure you can imagine, the meal of his life. And yet, when the farmer returned to the countryside, a slow dissatisfaction grew in him. And grew and grew. He lost the ability to conjure the memory of pleasure and could taste only his own hunger. Through a long winter of foul weather the farmer came to believe he had been a fool to eat so greedily and then be left to fast all year. He determined to return to the cabaret, but this time to nibble, to graze, to put a morsel in his mouth and savour its taste, to remove one note at a time from his handful of cash, and thence to visit the cabaret every season so that he might keep the sensation of fullness all year around. And so, when the farmer next went to the city—showered and shaved and togged out in a nearly new shirt—he exchanged words with the hotel concierge (this time as a man about town and not a bumpkin), went to the cabaret, sipped his cocktail, perused the menu and eventually, after the madame had cleared his glass and wiped his table and coughed loudly twice, he ran his finger down the list—past **Full Body incl. Head** and **Head/Neck/Shoulders** and **Full back** and **Bikini and Hand**—and finally ordered **Full Leg**. The madame was furious and tugged the menu from the farmer's hand, but the farmer did not care. He waited patiently and before long the leg arrived. Soft rounded thigh, strong kneecap, plump calf running to a thick ankle and broad foot. The farmer was ecstatic and, just as he had planned, he proceeded to commit each tendon and muscle, each arching of instep and pointing of toes, each callous and hair, deep into memory, and so returned to the countryside a different man. All who knew him said so—the postman, old Josie, his aunt on his mother's side. They spoke of a new maturity, solemn in its way, dignified. They all said that if any woman ever came to live in the countryside, he would certainly win her. And that was that. For years the farmer, at regular intervals, went to the city, stayed in the hotel, chatted to the concierge, visited the cabaret, ordered the leg (always the same one, mind), pleasured himself (and the leg, or so it seemed from the curling of the toes) and grew to exist in a rose-coloured haze, a plateau outside of reality, the realm of those who discover that most elusive of cycles— anticipation, climax, dream. Marked are such people by beauty, even in old age. The only giveaway is the shyness of their smiles in abstracted moments. And so it was with the farmer. Besotted, he took to buying the leg small, but expensive gifts from time to time—a silk garter, a silver anklet, a nail lacquer made from gold—all beautifully wrapped in tissue paper and ribbon. And, though never sought or expected, they were appreciated by the leg. Until one day the leg was gone. Have another, the madame said. But the man could not. Where was the leg, he cried. How could this happen?

I'll save you the rest… all love stories end the same way. The farmer returned to the countryside. He ploughed, he stemmed, he planted. He was the same, but he was bereft. He hardened his heart against love and lived happily ever after. A woman moved to the countryside. She was a great catch—a big car and not at all bad looking—and the farmer wooed her and caught her and married her. When interviewed for this story, he said he never thought of the leg anymore, and his wife said she believed him because there were no secrets between them, although she seemed a bit surprised when I mentioned the gifts her husband had given the leg.

[7] The Enormous Baby

Mr and Mrs Klotz were delighted at the birth of their son, Nicholas. After three daughters—all lovely—a son was an unspeakable triumph. They put a notice in the best newspaper and looked forward to having no more children:

> KLOTZ, LOUIS AND GRETTA (NÉE RATTRAY) ARE DELIGHTED TO ANNOUNCE THE BIRTH OF NICHOLAS TIBERIUS ON MARCH 1 IN THE NMH, A BROTHER FOR HONOR, EMILIA AND ROSAMUND.

The notice in the newspaper would become the first of many primary source documents later poured over by historians, cultural anthropologists and even novelists.

Nicholas was a good baby. He sucked heartily at breast, emptied his bowels regularly and slept easily. For a brief period of time (about a week) the future danced before the Klotzes in all its golden glory.

The first report of Nicholas's extraordinary growth rate appeared in the best newspaper in early April. People thought it was a seasonal joke:

> BABY BREAKS RECORD
>
> NICHOLAS TIBERIUS KLOTZ, THE ONLY SON OF LOUIS AND GRETA KLOTZ, HAS BROKEN THE CURRENT WORLD RECORD FOR WEIGHT AT ONE MONTH OLD. THE BABY'S WEIGHT WAS OFFICIALLY RECORDED AS 20KG AND WILL BE ENTERED IN THE NEXT EDITION OF THE GUINNESS BOOK OF RECORDS.

After three months Nicholas was the size of a chair, at five months he was the size of a writing desk, and by seven months he was the size of a bed. The headlines in the worst newspapers were not pleasant:

> MAMA MIA, WHAT YOU FEEDING THE FELLA?
>
> WATCH OUT—BABYZILLA ABOUT!
>
> KOLOSSAL KLOTZ KID

Mr and Mrs Klotz became unclear as to quite how delighted they were with their son Nicholas. After all, they were not the kind of people that peculiar things happened to. All the money they had saved for the girls' education, they spent on buying and converting an old sports hall into a new home. Friends and family chipped in to purchase a decommissioned lorry so that the family could take outings. Soon the government came on board, providing furniture for Nicholas made from zinc—functional but also light enough to move—as well as the use of the municipal swimming pool for bathing. The local Women's League ditched their Quilts for Africa project, instead making clothes for Nicholas from towels and blankets. The local supermarket came up with a scheme they called *Nosh for Nicholas*. For every €20 spent in store 1 cent was donated to Mr and Mrs Klotz towards food for their growing son. Many photos were taken of the Klotz family at this time. They depict an enormous happy baby with his parents crouched in front of him and his three sisters barely visible in the background.

Gradually life in the Klotz family got back to normal. Nicholas reached his full size at thirteen months and Louis and Gretta began to realise how lucky they were to have such a special son. Nicholas grew up to be a charming young man. He followed his father into the family business and, aside from the occasional appearances on TV shows and the deluge of books written about him, he went to lead a perfectly normal life. As for the girls, they spent their lives trying to get out from under some huge shadow. The shadow of what exactly they could never say.

[8] The Cloud

One day a cloud fell on the city. People had been speculating that something like this might happen but no one really believed it would. Initially there was panic. Lines of cars left the city in a slow colourful snake. Some people stayed, stocking up on canned food and water, waiting for the cloud to shift or break up. But a month later it was still there.

Some days the cloud was thin and fairly transparent and people went about their business as usual. Other days it was fat and fuliginous, as though it had swallowed foul air, and everyone had to stay indoors. People organised a march and walked through the streets chanting, 'Keep our cloud clean'. The government passed laws. No heavy industry within city limits. Everyone was happy, except the industrialists, who packed their bags and moved to another city. A year passed. The cloud became white and gauzy. People got used to it. They grew to like the misty view of the city, as though looking at the world through a muslin curtain. Those that had left the city came back and soon, apart from the closing of the airport and the reduced speed limits on the roads, everything returned to normal. Except it was a better normal. The cloud obscured the drabness of the city. All the ugly buildings and dark alleys were hidden in a veil. Children born at this time did not know that the world had ever looked different.

Every day the cloud changed in substance, shape and form. The changes were subtle, but people began to notice them more and more. Though it appeared to be a web of snow, the cloud was actually made of tiny droplets of ice crystals, so tiny that they floated in air. They could be clearly seen at sunset when, just for a moment, wavelengths of light scattered into a million colourful pieces before combining again to produce white.

Cautiously at first, and then with more confidence, people began making comments about the cloud. They said the same things, but in different ways. One man said that the cloud was a cotton honeycomb. Others said that the cloud resembled a leaf, or a spoked wheel, or the turrets of a castle if viewed from the side. A woman said that on cold days when the cloud wrapped around people on the street it gave the impression of halos. It was pointed out to the woman that this effect was caused by the refraction of the sun's rays on the surface of the cloud, but still, it awoke a vague memory of celestial times. A boy said that on hot days the ice crystals twisted themselves into shapes that made a fishbone pattern on the underbelly of the cloud.

Life in the city went on. People went to work and came home from work and fell in love and fell out of love and won things and lost things. But life had a new meaning. Even on dull days there was something to talk about. Private observations could be shared. People allowed it. And they took pleasure in expressing themselves carefully, searching for words, and leaving quiet space around words, so that words could be heard. Some days the cloud was a chandelier, other days it was a sea of silver dew, or a net in which the dimly visible disk of the moon was caught (nicely put, that).

Years passed, and then one day the city woke up and the cloud was gone. People had been speculating that something like this might happen but no one really believed it would. It turned out that each tiny ice crystal was in fact a piece of dust, around which water vapour had frozen, so that when the air warmed, all the tiny ice crystals simply disappeared, leaving behind all the pieces of dust. Initially there was panic. Lines of cars left the city in a slow colourful snake. Some people stayed, stocking up on canned food and water, waiting for the dust to shift or break up, but a month later the dust was still there. Children were amazed that the world could look so ugly. Everyone else adjusted. Heavy industry returned. The government created a Cloud Street from dry ice as a memorial to the cloud, but it wasn't very good. The view was more foggy than misty. Some people searched for that brief shimmer of rainbow light in the evenings while others thought about moving to another city, maybe in the mountains or along the coast. In the end most people stopped talking about the cloud and got back to talking about the weather (winter came with a vengeance, as they say).

[9] The Moon Shiner

This is the story of a man who was the first person to shine the moon [and the last]. It all happened a long time ago before life was in colour. [In homage to the man and the time I am going to tell this story in black and white.] It started on a salty cold day in March. It was salty because the man lived beside the sea and when the wind blew—as it did in March—it drew the salt off the sea and carried it inland for at least a mile. There were never any cases of hyponatremia among people who lived along the coastline. I digress. That day—that salty day in March—the man was mopping the floor in the juvenile delinquent detention centre as was his wont [but not his want, he wanted to be a museum attendant] when he saw the reflection of the moon in a bucket of water. The water—in the man's own words—was thin like cold coffee, but the moon—again in the man's own words—was caught in it. Looking into the bucket the man had the distinct impression that the moon was a little dull, that it had lost its lustre, that it was not at all as bright as it had been when he was a boy. Holding his mop in his hand he looked up at the sky and it was then that he got the idea. The man—I probably should have mentioned this earlier—was very resourceful [when his wife died leaving a new-born baby he got a new wife straight away]. And so he set about collecting all the old broom handles he could find so that his mop could reach the moon. It only took him four years and seven months. He attached the broom handles together with bolts and laid them across the sea in sections so as not to bother his neighbours. The salt of the sea made the wood of the broom handles as light as air and so the man was able, with the help of his new wife and his neighbours, to connect all the sections of broom handles together and make an extremely long mop to shine the surface of the moon. At first the effect was subtle—the moon was a little brighter—but soon, with nightly shining and improved technique, the effect was noticeable— the moon shone as bright as bone. Across the globe people were thrilled. Lovers danced all night in great stripes of moonlight. Children skipped in the yards of empty schools. Old folks walked down alleyways at midnight just for the hell of it. The man became a cause célèbre and a sepia photograph of him holding the mop handle became instantly iconic. The delight lasted a whole month before the complaints began. At first just the odd cranky letter in a newspaper but soon there were BRING BACK THE DARK protests and strikes by night-shift workers. There was even an attempt by an extremist group to make a brush handle long enough to paint the moon black. In one afternoon, the President went from being an exponent of shining the moon to being a detractor of shining the moon. There were two separate press conferences. In the first press conference he said: *The light of the moon will burn away darkness and fear for all people in all time.* [It was quite rousing.] In the second press conference he said: *All people in all time need darkness since only in fear can people feel safe.* [It was very rousing.] When a reporter [a rookie reporter] accused the President of contradicting himself, he replied: *I believe in the set and not the sub-set. The set is the moon. Shining is the sub-set. To focus attention on a sub-set instead of a set is to have a narrow view. I do not have a narrow view.* [This was extremely rousing and many people began to wear T-shirts with amusing slogans on them relating to sets and sub-sets.] Then everyone forgot about the moon and life returned to normal. The man chopped up the broom sticks for firewood and was never cold again. He resumed his job in the juvenile delinquent detention centre and when asked by a bright sixteen-year-old convict [a bit too bright in my opinion] if the experience had changed him, the man said no, except that when he was mopping the halls he avoided looking into the bucket of water. According to the young convict the man also said: *Confronted with the blackness of the universe man feels that which he cannot know as a dark emptiness in his soul. The white strings of the mop, pushing up into the firmament, were, for a brief time, an embodiment of that deepest of human desires, to reach the impossible*—but I don't believe this.

The End

A you I speak to

for Kevin Hart

There's a you I speak to most days
and most hours of most days,

agnostic days. On a morning walk
I pause. A muscled gum

bulges, twisted over the stooped
fence. I skirt corners, look up

through fractal branches posed,
against the kind of blue that overlooks

the bay. Another corner, and for fifty
metres the wind walks with me,

tuning the percussion of the leaves, then
stops. And I find myself saying

you, and asking who or what
I mean—the genii of the place; the day—

dark stars; whatever other planets
circle them; the hour still open;

or perhaps, the habit of something nearly
missed; that excess—at the edge of sense.

Anne Elvey

The Price of Flowers
John Siberry

He rode into town at eleven. He was crippled by three in the afternoon.

Before the Honda's engine was cold, he had sucked dry two pints of Stella Artois. Five pints of Heineken followed and three Jose Cuevera tequilas with lemon and salt chased the Heinekens. He crunched four packets of Planters roasted peanuts. He had never visited Mexico but said, 'Viva Mexico,' to the lone barman in Horgan's Bar and drained the last silver threads of tequila.

Outside, sunlight made him squint and he struggled to find the ignition switch of his motorcycle. He finally strapped his jacket to the saddle. Someone on the street may have heard the Honda's gears clash as he headed into the narrow roads beyond the town. He collided with a tractor at a crossroads where foxgloves flourished on the roadside banks. While he was airborne, he stared at the sun. His legs struck the road first, and his body followed as best it could. Apart from being crippled, he was unharmed. There was a valley to his north and the town to the south but never the opposite.

Rarely one to curse, even in front of animals, the farmer said shite, dismounted from his injured tractor and began to walk to a farmhouse to call for help. It was his first crash and he felt excited. He wondered if his insurance would cover the cost of repairs to the tractor. The roads were deserted and as always, the farmer used his cap to mop more sweat from his forehead. Ewes and some lambs had looked up at the sound of the collision but now grazed again.

On their way to the accident site, the ambulance crew of two paramedics travelled in silence and both men felt the lethargy of animals, sheep mostly, grazing along the crest of the ridge looking towards the mountains. The cab was warm, even with the windows down. They talked about the lapis lazuli shadows creased on the mountains and the man in the passenger's seat began to recall his recent holiday on the island of Lanzarote. He and his girlfriend had stuffed their cameras full of lunar landscapes and lewd, spectacular flowers. 'Like the surface of the moon,' he said and he explained how they were not permitted to leave the vehicle; this was to protect the 'unique and delicate terrain' of that part of the island. 'Barren and dusty as Mars,' the passenger said and though the sudden change of location amused the driver, he stayed quiet; they had worked together for over four years and he liked his colleague. The driver pointed to the ironwork of whitethorn bushes and occasionally to a sloe bush not yet in fruit. Their last call had involved two dead bodies and one uninjured, though now car-shy, Scotch terrier.

He crawled on his stomach, away from the Honda's broken bones. Soft tar damped the clinking of his belt buckle. Banners of foxglove arced up from thick moss and he wanted desperately to reach them. Below his waist he sensed a new void. He heard a lark. He had once tried to hear the bells of a foxglove chime but heard only the mechanical drone of insects, or something. Now he heard a sound he had not heard before but knew he would hear it forever.

He began to feel cold but his eyes still ravished the flowers.

Several minutes later a man shouldering a scuffed backpack stopped to examine the pool of oil on the road, the two machines and the man on his stomach.

'Ola. You make a fall?' the man said. He carried a peeled length of stick across his shoulders like a crucifix and drank from a scuffed goatskin about two thirds full of Rioja. The stranger offered the goatskin to the man on the road but the man said he never wanted to see another drink. The traveller shrugged, swallowed more wine and said he was from Galicia, a place similar in many ways to where they were now. 'There is much rain and the people still go to church,' he said. He spoke of shepherds and goats among acorns and the vicious loves of small villages. Taking an oatmeal biscuit from a shoulder bag, he offered some to the man at his feet who declined the offer; then the Galician sat on the bank's dry moss to eat the biscuit and to float his eyes over the ditches and warm grass.

The motorcyclist propped himself on one elbow and watched the Galician.

The Galician pointed to the insulted tractor, 'a Zetor, from the eastern bloc. Zetor. Now a wounded bull.'

The motorcyclist had not considered his nemesis before now and so allowed his gaze to caress the tractor's reddish orange paintwork, its oil-smeared engine and the geometrical carving of the rear tyres' hot rubber. The exhaust pipe, he saw, stood charred against the blue sky.

'This tractors are very strong, yes, but not lasting very long. The metal is not so good,' the Galician informed him.

The motorcyclist tried to nod.

An unseen sheep bleated maybe four times before the hot silence slumped down again.

The Galician began to sing, a sound like a trail of wood smoke from the grate of his throat. His eyes were closed.

'Turn left here,' the paramedic beside the driver said.

The ambulance turned but both saw their mistake, again.

'This place is unbelievable,' the driver said agitatedly, trying to reverse. He switched off the engine.

They sat in silence until the passenger said, 'I just thought of something.'

The driver looked at him; he had never seen his assistant look so grave. 'This is hardly the time?'

'It's important.'

The driver gazed into the trembling air. 'Will it take long? This accident we need to...'

'It might take forever, Mike,' the passenger said solemnly.

The Galician's voice changed timbre to that of vines in a shy breeze, then dropped to a stream of a trickle. A bee tried to silence him; the bee failed.

To the injured man on the road, the Galician appeared as a singing statue, the bearded mouth's dark bronze pouring honey into the air. Resting on his shoulders, the stick turned his dark profile into a crucified Christ.

The motorcyclist crawled forward for another twenty five or twenty six centimetres, his shoulders a rusted axle on which the body slowly turned. He wanted to crawl over continents, until his body was worn down to a toe or a single hair: the thought elated him. Pebbles like tiny teeth became embedded in his hands.

The Galician walked slowly to the tractor, climbed onto it and emitted a clacking, chugging sound of tractor engine. He laughed to himself. 'These ones are destroyers of the earth,' he said, gripping the machine's steering wheel.

The man on the road did not look up but leaned on both hands as the foxgloves drew closer.

'This is bad, real bad. What happens if we can't find the accident, we'll look like morons?' the ambulance driver said.

But his passenger was already talking. 'One day a guy, two years younger than me, spent the morning boozing. He went to the boozer early in the day, which was unusual for him. But apart from the heat, there was another reason for him going into a bar so early.'

'Which way here?' the driver said impatiently.

'Left,' his assistant said.

'Fuck this,' the driver said.

'The reason he went into the bar was because he'd argued with his brother about who should look after their old man who was crippled with rheumatism. Crippled. He left his motorbike outside the boozer and intended to walk home. He didn't believe in driving while drunk.'

The driver interjected, 'the bit of drunk driving seldom does much harm. Is it a right or left here?

'Right will do nicely. Anyway, this man had heard about drunk driving and knew the consequences.'

'This road looks a bit more promising,' the driver said, accelerating.

'Looks the same to me,' the passenger said. 'So, he'd heard all the horror stories. But he still put down seven pints and three tequilas, a lot for that hour of the day. All he had in his guts was a few packets of peanuts.'

'I go on my pilgrimage now, again,' the Galician said. The motorcyclist then heard about a journey over mountains, through snow-clogged passes, to the heat of the plains and buzz of insects and sunsets like floating scraps of flame. And who knows, maybe some fun with female pilgrims, the crucified man joked.

Until the Galician's hand tapped on the motorcyclist's helmet, the motorcyclist had forgotten it was still on his head. A moonless night had begun to spread slowly upwards from his buckled legs. He felt colder. But he had reached the roadside now and stretched his right arm towards the nearest stem of foxglove, gripped the heavy green column and felt fibres crack like glass on his skin. He recalled his past, crushed pictures of factory work and dinners at his parents' table.

He thrust the flower into the sky and heard their bells chime, all at once.

'Adios,' the crucified man said.

'He was twisted by drink and maybe that's why he chose to take the bike. His judgement was gone. He was lost,' the assistant paramedic said as they drove.

'There should be a map in this ambulance,' the driver said. 'An ordnance survey map of the area. This is ridiculous.'

The passenger continued, 'he loved nothing more than biking on a sunny day, drink or no drink. So he mounted up, totally pissed of course, and drove into the countryside.'

They passed people walking quickly and even running along the road.

'Look. I think this could be it,' the driver said urgently.

But his assistant barely noticed, 'he was pissed as a happy monkey. Next thing, a tractor crosses his path. Bang. Bye-bye legs, forever.'

'This is it,' the driver said. 'I can see some commotion up ahead. That was some fucking run-around.'

'He was my brother, the man on the bike. Crippled from the waist down. He had a bunch of foxgloves in his hand when the crew found him. Apparently it had taken the two pricks in the ambulance ages to reach him,' the passenger said and reached for a pair of latex gloves.

'You never told me. That was rough, sorry,' the driver said distractedly. 'You never know, about these fucking things, do you? There's some chewing gum there if you want it.'

'This is the crash, alright,' the assistant said, leaning forward. 'Get ready.'

gorse no. 2 | art in words

FEATURING

Claire-Louise Bennett • Dylan Brennan • Alan Cunningham
Brian Dillon • Rob Doyle • S.J. Fowler • Tristan Foster
Hugh Fulham-McQuillan • Jonathan Gibbs • Niven Govinden
Matthew Jakubowski • Christodoulos Makris • Mira Mattar
Colm O'Shea • Catherine O'Sullivan • Simon Reynolds • Tim Smyth
Susan Tomaselli • Lies Van Gasse

285 PAGES | ISBN 978-0-9928047-1-8

www.gorse.ie

Colorless Tsukuru Tazaki and His Years of Pilgrimage
by **Haruki Murakami** (Vintage Books, 2014, £20)

Triangle
by **Hisaki Matsuura** (Dalkey Archive Press, 2014, £10.50)

I don't know whose idea Haruki Murakami was, but it seems to be paying off. When his thirteenth novel came out in Japan last year, it sold a million copies in two weeks. There were queues at midnight, reviews by morning. It's a weird phenomenon, one that you sense this book's protagonist would have little time for. Tsukuru Tazaki is another of Murakami's ascetic types. He lives in a studio apartment, takes his job seriously, swims routinely, never travels. He entertains few bad habits, fewer guests, and for the longest time he was happy to wear any old digital watch. When his father died, Tsukuru inherited his beautiful antique Heuer. He enjoys 'the weight and heft of it', he enjoys its 'mechanical whir'. This is a novel about the passage of time.

On his fourth date with Sara, Tsukuru opens up about his childhood. In high school he had been part of a close-knit group of friends—two girls, three boys, five thoroughly wholesome archetypes. They'd to do everything together—hiking, fishing, studying, the works—and they wouldn't hang out in twos or threes lest it somehow destroy their special chemistry. Needless to say, nobody fucked; but Tsukuru got fucked over. One day his friend Ao told him that none of the group ever wanted to see him again. He offered no explanation and sixteen years later Tsukuru remains none the wiser. This abandonment was traumatic. Tsukuru turned in on himself, allowing death to 'envelop him in its embrace for nearly half a year'. By the time he came through it, he had hardened in such a way that even his physical appearance had changed.

Despite his success at home and abroad, Murakami claims to be the outcast of Japanese literature. Posturing notwithstanding, it's true that his work is—or has been—qualitatively different to the work of other Japanese writers. Taking Raymonds Chandler and Carver as models, Murakami created a form of Japanese that mimics the structures of everyday American speech. Starting out, he used to write first drafts in English, then translate them into Japanese. His early work is deadpan, hard-boiled, heavily ironised. For Otsuku Eishi, Murakami's writing is 'like American literature translated into Japanese'.

In the hardened post-traumatic figure of Tsukuru, who is at one point described in explicitly linguistic terms, we find the embodiment of Murakami's distant and unhomely prose. 'Slowly he grew used to this new self. It was like acquiring a new language, memorising the grammar.' Yet the world remains at one remove from him. 'Colors he'd once seen appeared completely different, as if they'd been covered by a special filter.' Sara spots it too. She says that when they slept together, 'it felt like you were somewhere else'. She refuses to keep seeing him until he discovers why his friends abandoned him, attributing his distant performance in bed to a psychological 'blockage' caused by their unexplained rejection of him. She locates for him his former friends, one of whom is dead. Then she plans the three legs of his pilgrimage, helps him to renew his passport and puts him in touch with local car rental agents. She does an awful lot for such a new friend, and forces him to do still more.

It is difficult to overstate the amount of plot in this novel. One turns page after page of storyline only to arrive at *more* storyline. It's awful, it takes ages, and its revelations ruin whatever was interesting about the story to start with. An unease with the unknown has become characteristic of Murakami's later period, where what had once been incoherent is now, in Christopher Tayler's terms, 'coherently incoherent'. The deadpan is gone too, replaced by a misty weatherman-lyricism. These days even office furniture puts his narrators in mind of 'a fine rain falling under a midnight sun'. At last, Tsukuru understands that he is not a bad person. He has become 'unblocked', less hardened, more in touch with his emotions. His story is an allegory of the journey made by the prose in which it is told. It is not a happy story.

*

Neither is *Triangle*, though it is in parts more interesting. On a sparsely lit street one evening, its first-person narrator puts Hikoro in a taxi. He is happy to get rid of her. Otsuku is a former drug addict and he sleeps around. He has no steady job, living instead on the dollar of the husbands of the women who come and go. He is the mirror image of Tsukuru Tazaki—at heart they are both loners.

After seeing Hikoro off, Otsuku takes a walk down some unfamiliar streets and ends up bumping into Sugimoto, a shady character from his past who convinces him to visit a man about a job. The pair make their way through a dark octagonal house until they finally come face-to-face with Koyama. Though his 'cold, reptilian eyes' certainly suggest it, for now it's not clear that Koyama is a bad guy. He persuades Otsuku to watch a film.

Triangle is Hisaki Matsuura's first novel to be translated into English. Though there are no conspicuous wristwatches here, it is for that no less a novel about the passage, or non-passage, of time. Koyama comes right out and says it: 'What is your concept of time?' He doesn't wait around for an answer either, instead entering into what Otsuku describes as a 'meandering, unbalanced monologue' in which he rubbishes linear and circular concepts of time in favour of his own theory of infinite 'nows' all existing within each 'now'. *Triangle* is a novel with a radically destabilised chronology; everything that happens, happens at once. Memory and premonition are synonymous, and the line dividing subject and object is blurred at best. This is a mixed blessing in narrative terms. It affords the author so many opportunities to pull the rug from under us that soon we simply step aside and watch a rug whisked around to no effect.

The film Otsuku watches is described in detail. 'The structure was simple—scenes showing the habits of various insects inter-spliced with scenes of explicit pornography.' What's most important here is the girl. Her name is Tomoe, and she provides the novel not only with its most significant character, a mantis-like figure whose 'syrupy cries of sex' echo through Otsuku's mind, but also its structuring principle. We learn early on that Koyama is a nationally revered calligrapher. What takes a little longer to be revealed is that *tomoe* refers to a spiral-like character in Japanese script. Otsuku finally understands his fascination with the curve of Tomoe's armpits, with 'Tomoe's body floating silently on air'. She is a symbol of herself. 'When Tomoe's hair spreads across the water,' says Koyama, 'that is also a written character.' If Murakami's early work represents an effort to put writing at a distance from its object, Tomoe is precisely the opposite. In the figure of Tomoe, writing is reconciled with its object. She is a utopian situation, the final realisation of a dream centuries-held that humanity might one day rediscover a pre-Babelic language, a universal system of communication capable, in Umberto Eco's terms, 'of expressing the nature of things through a kind of homology between things and words'. Just be careful what you wish for. She eats the narrator's head off.

—KEVIN BREATHNACH

Waiting for the Bullet

by Madeline D'Arcy (Doire Press, 2014, €12)

The narrator of 'Clocking Out', the lead story in Madeleine D'Arcy's debut collection *Waiting for the Bullet* recounts a recurring dream where she is walking down Oxford Street, 'and the thing falls out of me and everybody in the street sees it dragging along behind me on the footpath on its fleshy string and I don't even notice'. 'Clocking Out' is the story of a pregnant woman abandoned to the silence of those around her: 'Nobody said anything to me when I started getting big. Nobody said a word.' This is harrowing, emotionally-charged territory, plenteous with opportunities for a writer to get things wrong. In attempting to give voice to the voiceless, there is always the danger that a writer may, paradoxically, engage in silencing of a different sort by taking up position between reader and characters, intruding upon the story. D'Arcy, fortunately, knows when to let her characters do the talking. Here, she wisely chooses a first person narrative and then stays out of our way. What results is a story devoid of sentimentality that delivers the human aspect of the political. 'I was in pain. It came out. I hated it...' the narrator tells us, '... It was like a dead dog on a leash. I had to bite the stringy bit off or it would drag along the ground after me forever until I died.'

This collection, published by Doire Press, contains twelve stories set in Cork, New York, and London where D'Arcy lived and worked as a solicitor and legal editor for a number of years. Among the themes explored are the human capacity for self-destruction, and our propensity to squander, in particular the way in which we squander love. D'Arcy's gaze falls not so much on the quest for love, but on the more complex, and arguably more interesting, question of what people do with love after they've found it. The male narrator of 'An Under-rated Emotion' is dating a younger woman who is 'smart', 'sexy', 'beautiful' and 'puts up with [him]'. And putting up with him is no mean feat. He isn't, it's fair to say, any great catch, and as readers we know something his girlfriend doesn't: he's had a vasectomy. There seems little doubt as to who has got the better deal here, and yet we witness the narrator going in like a wrecking ball, running from the happiness that's within his grasp. It's a theme revisited in the collection: this wanton turning away from happiness. With this narrator, as with a number of the other characters who populate D'Arcy's stories, I was put in mind of dogs chasing cars; yes, there's that initial flurry of pursuit, but they come to a halt, confused and bewildered, should a car actually stop.

In 'Salvage', Vincent is in his late thirties, recently separated, and on the hunt for a bedsit in post-boom Cork. Not a man over-burdened with self awareness, he professes to be amazed at 'the way people sow the seeds of their own destruction'. I was entertained by his tussles with his new landlord's cat, and by his hapless efforts to contact his ex: 'Her last text said, 'Please stop ringing me and texting me,' so I email her instead…' Yet alongside the humour, the reader is invited to observe the twin wrecks of the narrator's failed marriage and career—and the unfolding parallel narrative of the Japanese tsunami, the reportage of 'dazed, homeless people' who find, suddenly, that 'the places they lived in are unrecognisable'. Like Eddie in 'The Wolf Note', who defies his wife to go drinking with the lads, things started out lightly enough, but now we've 'gone over to the dark side'.

While the stories may be sweetened with humour, they are not prettified or sanitised. D'Arcy does not sidestep the bleakness of her characters' situations, but juxtaposes light and dark, using humour to coax the reader forward. In the Hennessy Award-winning story 'Is this like Scotland?' Fintan has brought his wife, Annika, to visit rural Cork where he grew up, but the trip is not turning out as he'd hoped. I laughed at his efforts to converse with his Swedish in-laws, and at the confusion in the pub when, in an effort to explain his hunger, he tells his father-in-law he 'might have worms'. But a deepening sadness unfolds as the visit serves only to highlight the extent of the mismatch between him and his wife. In 'Housewife of the Year', the writing, as well as being funny, is also sharply satirical. 'You needed about eight children to win…' the narrator tells us, and her mother 'had only five… But my father died suddenly, soon after she posted the entry form. She was a widow then; that balanced things out.'

In 'The Fox and the Placenta' Marilyn is on the verge of giving birth, walking 'naked in a cowboy mode' around her front room. She is assisted by two midwives—one from China, one from Derry—and by Brendan, devoted, but possibly not the father. There is plenty of scope for comedy here and D'Arcy avails of it all, yet the story never crosses the line into farce. Even as we laugh we are aware of menace lurking outside the walls—the shadowy presence of another man, and urban foxes on the prowl, 'hordes of them, packs that come out when daylight turns to night'.

D'Arcy has an ear for dialogue, a way of capturing the nuances in what people say, as well as in what they don't. She creates intimacy between her characters and her readers; we lean in and listen. It's a skill that extends to how her characters communicate via text message, as in the entertaining and poignant exchanges between Eddie and his wife in 'The Wolf Note'. The wolf note of the story's title is a reference to cellos, where the vibrations of the cello's body and the vibrations of a string may cancel each other out. The better the cello, the more problematic the wolf note may be. There's a rich seam of music running through the collection and the stories often incorporate snippets of song and verse, with lines from nursery rhymes and references to pop hits and ballads woven through the narratives. In 'Hole in the Bucket' the sweetly-sinister verses of an old folk song, circular and repetitive, provide a backdrop to the narrator's denial. And there it is again, that juxtaposing of light and dark, of sweet and bitter, a hallmark of this assured and carefully crafted collection whose stories will follow you around long after you've stopped laughing.

—DANIELLE MCLAUGHLIN

X
by Vona Groarke (The Gallery Press, 2014, €11.95)

In her latest collection of poetry, X, Vona Groarke throws the word 'love' around with abandon. Anyone trained to cull poems of big unearned abstractions can't help but scare at the intemperance. Are we suddenly all agreed on what love is? X's title is the algebraic symbol used to signify unknown quantities, yet one of its poems, 'The Road', relegates love to the category of only too well-*known* quantities by means of a handful of adjectives:

> the way love is: correct, plausible,
> willful; awfully sure of itself.

By strewing the name of 'love' with such casual frequency—conjuring it only to pass on from it—X sets love aside. It frees itself to examine what is available to the self above and beyond that measure of a life spent falling in love with, seducing, caring for, keeping or losing another person. X strikes out for the mysterious realm of unfocused desire—'as if longing could be an end in itself'—and the even less-well understood realm of desire's lack, the latter imagined in one glittering poem as a moment in a doorway in a strange city where 'noirish rain and teeming lives' have 'nothing to do with you,'

> ...pronounce themselves
> above and beyond any word you care to choose

> Of which you are unaccountably innocent.
> You could hold out your open hand, let it fill
> with what is happening. But you don't.

An accomplished formalist, Groarke has already proven what she can make with words in poems like 'An American Jay' (*Spindrift*, 2009) and 'Flight' (*Flight*, 2002). But in *X*, more than in earlier collections, formal hijinks are subservient to negotiating with the world, to figuring out what there is once the business of marrying, making a home and raising a family concludes or is cut short. The poems let loose little firecrackers of appalling emotion—betrayal, loneliness, unrequited lust—then work hard to move past these wormy horrors. The destination we're after here, it seems, is pleasure in middle age. The heart, in these poems, might learn 'to accept itself as autumnal' and earn the capacity to 'sit out weather people fret about'. And X does mine middle age for its real advantages: its earned intuition of the long length of a lifespan; its faith in the resilience earned through habit; its intensified pleasure in the sheerly sensual; its lessening reliance on witness. To describe Groarke's collection in the terms of such a journey risks making it sound like some kind of prolonged, lyrical, talkshow whoop of, 'You go, girl!' But X's comforts are slow-won and unreliable to the last, though admittedly an exhilarated opening-up to the universe is its most gorgeous note:

> to observe the fields of an afternoon,
> the way they chase each other down
> in the kind of blue that learned abstraction
> moons ago, how they resolve themselves
> into a love poem for no one in particular,
> written to be open, for the sake of openness,
> this night and every budding night inside.

Groarke's poetry has always been stubbornly concerned with the domestic and intimate. Even when she wrote about the 1916 Rising, it was to imagine the food consumed in the course of the siege, the dreams of the new republic rendered in the form of an ambitious kitchen ('Imperial Measure', *Flight*). Throughout her career, she has seemed almost improperly fascinated with the house as a metaphor, and indeed with the house as house, pushing the domestic space as theme and figure to what one would have presumed to be exhaustion (and possibly exhausting some readers) in her second collection, *Other People's Houses* (1999). In X she somehow finds new things to say about the architecture of the domestic space and how we live in it; and in particular, she turns her eye on the back garden. Groarke's garden is a record of the years, the tulips in it alluding to tulips past:

> Those black tulips that never put forth
> so much as a single bloom
> …
> and every tulip planted since
> a righting of the weight of darkness

Her garden is a negotiation between what the individual has been able to choose or control and what has been allotted to her: 'the azalea I earthed / and the rowan I did not'. It is one response to the questions posed in the volume's opening poem, questions about whether self-sufficiency might equate to pointlessness. Is a life spent building a life the waste of a life? A garden exists for the sake of itself, and it matters deeply, for the breadth and the width of a garden. But Groarke's garden is also a landscape which experiences no particular love or rancour towards us, which bears our traces but cannot be expected to keep faith with those traces: 'soil / behind sleepers // will eventually rise to it / and all my scheme and wager / come undone'. It belies attempts elsewhere in the volume to attribute some measure of consciousness to things and places in order that we might not feel so alone in the world. If, in 'The White Year', 'two bridges on the same river / will have knowledge of each other,' (an assertion which is plainly true in some good sense), in 'The Garden as Music and Silence', it's only the poet who is given to 'imagine' that 'the blue of cornflowers / has knowledge / of gothic windows / and tapestried plainsong'.

It is right and proper that an honest poetic investigation of this nature should contain turnings-back, contradictions, uncertain gestures and a measure of what Derek Mahon called 'solving ambiguities'—and X does. But some of its mysteries seem less forgivable than others. A question like '[w]hat colour / is the colour of where / the last moon used to be?' feels like false profundity. The assertion that

> It should be easy to say
> the garden speaks
> with the silver of wood
> left out over winter
> in all weathers.

> But it is not.

is smoke and mirrors. But it's hard to take Groarke much to task for these moments that don't hit the spot, since it's exciting to see her striking out beyond the precisions and certainties of her earlier poetry. Perhaps these moments are pitfalls of the laudable task of writing about the very things of which you are most uncertain. Perhaps it's only right to give a jolt to the reader who trusts you to lead them somewhere solid to sit and think, or somewhere with moving parts that work. X is concerned with the desiring human in a guise—that of the middle-aged woman, alone—often passed over by the simplistic script laid out by our cultural world. With it, Groarke joins those who have escorted Irish poetry to realms where it seemed not so inclined to go, poets like Eavan Boland,

Eiléan Ní Chuilleanáin and Medbh McGuckian, who also happen to be women.

And love? Groarke remarks once more on the 'gold of love' in the final lines of her book, writing about a portrait by the Danish painter Vilhelm Hammershoi, with whose subtle and mystery-ridden palette she has much in common. Whether the 'gold of love' is the divine gold of a religious icon, dreaming of heaven, or gaudy and false as gilt, there it is at the end of *X*'s investigation: 'not being, maybe never being, / subdued' by all that is true apart from it.

—AILBHE DARCY

Talking to Ourselves
by Andrés Neuman (Pushkin Press, 2014, £8.99)

The Insufferable Gaucho
by Roberto Bolaño (Picador, 2014, £14.99)

'All writers learn from the dead,' Margaret Atwood writes. Grab any book, and this tuition can be more or less obvious, as well as more or less pleasant. In the best case, it will give you an itch to read more. At worst it'll make you feel lost. Most of the time, it's a little bit of both.

This spring saw the English-language publication, and re-publication, of works from two authors who make conversation with the dead its own art form. Roberto Bolaño died in 2003, leaving behind enough material to keep his publishers and translators busy for years to come (*The Insufferable Gaucho* was first published in English in 2010 by New Directions). The younger author—also a transatlantic émigré—Andrés Neuman, is very much alive. In their writing they continue to not only speak to each other but—it seems—with every author that's ever made an impression on them.

In *Talking to Ourselves*, Neuman uses three voices and parallel chronologies to tell the story of a small family in crisis: Mario, terminally ill with cancer, takes his son on a road trip to give him one lasting happy memory. Mario's voice-recordings to his son—made after their return—sit alongside the son's immediate impressions during the journey, and the thoughts of his mother, Elena, documented at home during and after the trip. As the novel itself depends on the trip eventually coming to an end, the journey becomes a narrative stem: both an escape and a confrontation.

Neuman effectively uses this triangle of perspectives, making each reflect the story's core themes. They are three modes of language—speech, writing, inner monologues—and the sad and beautiful paradox lies in their isolation. These narratives are filled with concern for loved ones, yet they are also brutally honest about the intrinsic selfishness of love. Nobody understands this better than Elena, the mother. 'A child is literally an investment', she tells her appalled sister, and just like adults, children also 'speculate with their love [...] if I'm nice to Dad I'll have a few days of credit; if I'm nice to Mum the two of us can negotiate with him.' Elena holds illness by the hand. Through her, Neuman highlights love as always beginning with the self. Someone's need for you brings the gratification of being needed, and caring for a loved one in their suffering also comes with the awful relief of that suffering's potential end. All of this is love, and Neuman dwells in it with a clear prose which is also deeply sympathetic; it invites its readers to look into harsh mirrors without lapsing into cynicism. Perhaps this is the reason I find the sections narrated by the son, Lito, the weakest. Next to the self-deprecation and honesty of the others, even a child occasionally comes across as much too oblivious. Interestingly, these are also the only instances where Nick Castor and Lorenza Garcia's otherwise so elegant translation chafes at the seams.

Throughout *Talking to Ourselves*, Elena dedicates herself to reading, and we read along with her. Rather than a writer quoting favourites, this is the free association that comes with every first-read. She applies every line to her own situation, and the specificity of these small introductions makes the reading contagious.

It won't be news to readers of Bolaño to learn that a whole army of dead writers appear in *The Insufferable Gaucho*, translated by Chris Andrews. This is an oblique, and surprisingly fluid, combination of five stories, a lecture, and an essay. The result is seductive. Throughout, Bolaño continues to speak to other writers, some living, most of them dead. The second piece—which gives the collection its title—is a reply to the story 'The South' by Borges, and the final essay is a call of discontent aimed at idealised notions of Latin American literature, and why best-sellers sell.

Bolaño confuses me; his writing often overwhelms, and I have yet to find a definite reason why I keep returning to it. There's the posthumous-fame phenomenon, of course, but if anything that should put me off. There's an illusory simplicity in stories such as 'Police Rat', in which a rat working as a police officer investigates a murder in the sewers. It seems he's the only one seeking the truth, whilst the wider rat-community prefers to remain in the literal dark. The story appears neatly tied up on the level of pace and rhythm. Still, it continues to demand attention, perhaps another read. There's also, with Bolaño, a desire to say it all, say it in the way that will hit hardest, and say it now. The lecture 'Literature+Illness=Illness' has anger, irony and despair shooting through it like a transatlantic jet-plane. Individual references may get lost in the momentum; you won't catch all of it, but it's undoubtedly a unique experience. Above all, you'll know for sure that here was someone who really did have things to say, and there was never time for beating around the bush.

As with the rest of Bolaño's work, it's difficult to be done with *The Insufferable Gaucho*. His lecture on illness begins with a fateful medical appointment, then heads into a ridiculously huge lift which will take the author to a series of tests. Within the walls of this lift Bolaño manages to squeeze the word and the idea of 'illness' for all its worth, holding it up to the light and testing it from unexpected angles. There's hardly a more appropriate vehicle for such a journey. The lift goes up and down endlessly; it is meant to be revisited.

Literary pantheons are only interesting if they say something about the personal and the specific—if they, as well as talking to themselves, also speak to the reader's day-to-day reality. Both of these books exemplify how our night skies of literature come together—a conglomeration of where we've been, by whom we've been taught, and in which language—speaking as much through representation as through negligence. Heavy with titles and names, writing like this can become dense and alienating. A happy alliance comes to depend on how well the backdrop of the dead is balanced with a creative present, allowing true reflection. Necessity, I think, is key: both these books turn to other books when in need. At her husband's death bed, Neuman's character Elena picks one book after the other, reading hungrily, using books in whatever way they help her survive. Unsurprisingly, one of the texts she picks up is about illness, an essay published in Spanish in 2003 by Roberto Bolaño. It was, supposedly, the last book he prepared for publication before his death.

—JESSICA JOHANNESSON GAITÁN

How To Be Both
by Ali Smith (Hamish Hamilton, 2014, £12.99)

Somewhere in the middle of Ali Smith's Booker-shortlisted *How to be both*, a British family visit a 15th-century fresco in Ferrara, Italy. Carol, the mother, muses on the relationship between experiencing a piece of art and knowing its chronological history. Sometimes, she tells George (her very teenage, very uninterested daughter), the underdrawings for the paintings are later discovered to be radically different from the finished work. 'But the first thing we see… and most times the only thing we see, is the one on the surface. So does that mean it comes first after all? And does that mean the other picture, if we don't know about it, may as well not exist?' The novel is divided into two separate but interlinked parts, one part dealing with George and her mother, the other with the painter of the Palazzo Schifanoia that they have come to visit—Francesco del Cossa, a real historical figure. The story you read will start with one part or the other—both called Part One—depending on the copy of the book that you have selected. To be sure, no reader is an entirely detached critic, but in this case Smith has denied us even the pretence of a neutral reading, making us ask if we can ever truly separate ourselves from our past to read something objectively. To quote Carol again, who is prone to asking questions that resonate throughout the book: 'Which comes first? What we see or how we see?'

As if to prove her point, the reader witnesses this conversation through the opaque filter of time passed. It is now six months later, and three months since George's mother died suddenly—leaving George to deal with her absence, and the painful presence of her memory: 'That was then. This is now. It's February now… Her mother's not now anything.' George is an endearing, brainy, and somewhat odd 16-year-old with a pedantic obsession with grammar, and it is her consciousness that dominates this half of the novel. Conversations, images and turns of phrase all serve as trapdoors into earlier memories, and, naturally enough, the shadow of grief hangs over her present-day experiences, so that what we read is hybrid of then and now, a conversation between 'the George from before her mother dies' and 'the George from after'. Interwoven with her memories, however, are touchingly plausible interactions with her father and brother; speculations about art, empathy, history, and pornography; and moments of charming tenderness with H, her school friend who makes her feel 'in an undeniable present tense'.

The other Part One is set in an even less concrete space, somewhere between memory and experience. Here, the spirit of the artist del Cossa—bodiless and voiceless, but with a fully functioning sense of humour—is dragged from the 15th century to the present day. Del Cossa, it transpires, was born female, but lived publicly as a man so as to be allowed to work as an artist. She in turn mistakes George for a boy, and as she observes her from afar she is constantly reminded of her own past. Although Francesco's train of thought jumps back and forth in the same erratic manner as George's, her story is a surprisingly traditional *Künstlerroman*—except for the fact that she is biologically female. In a refreshing twist on a classic trope, the women in the Bologna house of pleasure teach del Cossa the art of love in exchange for portraits, and show her that 'in the making of pictures and love—both—time changes its shape: the hours pass without being hours, they become something else, they become their own opposite, they become timelessness, they become no time at all'.

My copy of the book started with the modern-day part, and so the only story that can exist for me holds George at its centre. I cannot go back and read it the other way, knowing what I already know about the lonely-looking 'boy' that del Cossa is watching. In fact I almost don't feel qualified to talk about the other version because I have never read it—worse still, can never read it. For me, a story starting with Francesco might as well not exist; we can never, as Carol laments, 'get beyond ourselves' to know the other story. All the same, I can't help but feel that George's story is the meatier, more engaging of the two. Francesco's part seems a little like an add-on, or a side note, and struggled to live up to the promise of the first half. In a book so full of echoes and duplicates, and with so many parallels between George's life and Francesco's, the lack of equilibrium between the two halves is a little disconcerting.

But then, I wonder whether that isn't the idea. In another imagined exchange with an Italian renaissance artist (Parmigianino, painter of the original 'Self Portrait in a Convex Mirror') John Ashbery eventually becomes disillusioned with his vision of the world as a single, perfect whole. If the work of art is perfectly unified within itself, it must be separate from the world, and not truly reflective of it: 'a globe like ours, resting / On a pedestal of vacuum'. Maybe Smith has deliberately made the two halves uneven, co-existent but not cohesive, and filled it with so many flashbacks, asides and contradictions in order to create a work that is, as George describes del Cossa's vastly diverse fresco, 'so full of life happening that it's actually like life'.

If this all sounds dreadfully complex, please bear with me. It's difficult to discuss the fascinating topics raised without straying into the annoyingly theoretical. In fact, unlike John Ashbery, Smith's writing is refreshingly simple. Her loose, seemingly spontaneous style makes every flashback and flash-forward read like a perfectly natural progression. Or, as Francesco tries to tell George, 'roads that look set to take you in one direction will sometimes twist back on themselves without ever seeming anything other than straight.' Moreover, Smith asks all these questions about death, time, memory and identity in such an offhand manner that they appear a mere supplement to the very real humans she creates. As well as sardonic, generous, charming George, I am left with a crisp impression of her impish, argumentative mother. Carol is a warm and vibrant creature, to use a variation of another of Francesco's analogies, pulled like a fish from her daughter's memories and straight into the mind of the reader.

For a school project on empathy, George's friend H suggests that they should imagine they were in del Cossa's head. This, coupled with the fact that

Francesco's spirit speaks in a surprisingly modern idiom (phrases like 'just saying' crop up a lot), suggests that the painter might have been imagined by George herself. But del Cossa's memories are so vivid, and her observations on George so shrewd, that it's hard to imagine she exists only in George's mind. So does it matter if Francesco is the fruit of George's invention, or a spirit summoned from the 15th century? Must del Cossa, or George, be either male or female? Do we have to forget about the past in order to live in the present? Must we choose one explanation? The novel is a call for an acceptance of multiplicity as a part of life, and an uplifting and utterly enjoyable celebration of the multifarious forms of love and art and identity. True, we can only really experience one of the two stories on offer, but it's worth it for the multiple possibilities allowed us in return.

—LILY NÍ DHOMHNAILL

NOTES ON CONTRIBUTORS

Kevin Barry is the author of the International IMPAC Dublin Literary Award winning novel, *City of Bohane*. His debut short story collection, *There Are Little Kingdoms*—published by The Stinging Fly Press in 2007—earned him the Rooney Prize, while *Dark Lies The Island*, his second short story collection, won the 2013 Edge Hill Short Story Award. *Beatlebone*, a novel, will be published by Canongate in 2015.

Claire-Louise Bennett lives in the west of Ireland. 'The Lady of the House' was the 2013 winner of The White Review Short Story Prize. Her debut short-story collection, *Pond*, will be published by The Stinging Fly Press in 2015.

Kevin Breathnach is a writer and critic. His work has appeared in *The Dublin Review, The New Inquiry, The Irish Times, gorse* and elsewhere. He lives in Dublin.

Ron Butlin is an international prize-winning novelist and a former Edinburgh Makar/Poet Laureate. His most recent novel is *Ghost Moon* (Salt, 2014). 2015 will see the publication of his new collection *Scotland's Magic* (Polygon), and his first book of poetry for children, *Here Come the Trolls!* (Polygon).

Máirtín Coilféir is from Navan in County Meath. He lives in Dublin, where he teaches at UCD.

Ailbhe Darcy published her first full-length collection of poetry, *Imaginary Menagerie*, in 2011 with Bloodaxe. This autumn she toured Ireland presenting collaborative works with other poets as part of Steven Fowler's "Enemies" project.

Ted Deppe has lived in Ireland since 2000 and currently makes his home in Connemara. His five books of poetry include *Beautiful Wheel* (Arlen House, 2014) and *Cape Clear: New and Selected Poems* (*Salmon*).

Gavan Duffy lives in Dublin. He is a member of Platform One writers group and has previously published in *Crannog, South Bank Poetry, Stony Thursday, Poetry Porch* and forthcoming issues of *Poetry Ireland Review* and *New Irish Writing*.

Anne Elvey is author of *Kin* (Five Islands Press, 2014) and managing editor of *Plumwood Mountain: An Australian Journal of Ecopoetry and Ecopoetics*. She lives in Melbourne, Australia, and holds honorary appointments at Monash University and University of Divinity.

Oliver Farry was born and raised in County Sligo. He lives in Paris, where he works as a journalist, translator and editor.

Roderick Ford has won several poetry prizes and is currently working on his third collection. A new play, *The Threshold of Yellow,* should be ready shortly.

Erin Fornoff has performed her poetry at Glastonbury, James Taylor in concert, and Farmleigh House's "New Voices" with Hollie McNish and Hozier. Widely published, she won the 2013 StAnza Slam and was selected for the 2014 Poetry Ireland Introductions Series.

Andrew Fox was born in Dublin and lives in New York City. His first book, a collection of short stories entitled *Over Our Heads*, is forthcoming from Penguin Ireland in 2015.

Hugh Fulham-McQuillan is a doctoral researcher in psychology in Trinity College Dublin, and a writer. He was most recently published in *gorse*, and has work forthcoming in *Ambit* magazine.

Jessica Johannesson Gaitán grew up in Sweden and Colombia and is now based in Edinburgh. Her stories have appeared in *Witness Magazine, Gutter* and *Structo* and Issue 28 of *The Stinging Fly,* among others. She writes about fiction in translation at therookeryinthebookery.org.

Matthew Geden was born and brought up in the English Midlands, moving to Kinsale in 1990. His most recent book is *The Place Inside*, published by Dedalus Press.

Natalie Holborrow was 2013 second-prize winner of the Terry Hetherington Award and was commended for the Hippocrates Prize 2012 and Bridport Prizes 2010-12. She has recently completed her first poetry collection. She lives in Swansea.

Jillian Kring is a poet from Boston. She completed the MPhil in Creative Writing at Trinity College Dublin. She was a featured spoken-word poet at the Monday Night Echo, and is currently working on her first novel. jillian-kring.squarespace.com.

Dave Lordan's latest book is the poetry collection *Lost Tribe of the Wicklow Mountains* (*Salmon Poetry*). He has previously published another two poetry collections (*The Boy In The Ring, Invitation to a Sacrifice*) and a short-story collection (*First Book of Frags*). He guest-edited the Summer 2012 Issue of *The Stinging Fly*.

Danielle McLaughlin's short stories have appeared in various newspapers, journals and anthologies, most recently *The Fog Horn, The Penny Dreadful, The South Circular, Southword, The Irish Times* and *The New Yorker*. Her first collection will be published by The Stinging Fly Press in 2015.

Rachel McNicholl is a freelance translator based in Dublin. She studied German, Italian and French, worked as a language teacher and journalist, and lived in Zurich and Hamburg before returning to Ireland in 1997. Her latest translation project is a short story collection by Austrian author Nadja Spiegel, to be published by Dalkey Archive Press.

Lily Ní Dhomhnaill lives in Dublin and is Editorial Assistant at *The Stinging Fly*. She recently completed a degree in English and Spanish at Trinity College, Dublin, where she was a writer and editor for *tn2 Magazine*.

Michael Nolan (b. 1990) is from Belfast. He won the Avalon Prize for poetry in 2011 and completed the Creative Writing MA at Queen's University Belfast in 2012. He has published several short stories, and his debut novella, *The Blame*, was published by Salt in June 2014

Deborah Rose Reeves was raised in Dublin and now lives in Portland, Oregon. This is her first published story.

Frank Schulz lives and writes in Hamburg, northern Germany. He is best known for his novel series *Hagener Trilogie* (1991, 2001, 2006), for which he won several literary awards. His first collection of short stories, *More Love: Tricky Stories*, appeared in 2010. In 2012 he was awarded the prestigious Kranichsteiner Literature Prize by the German Literature Fund. 'Bittersweet Nightshade' (from the above short story collection) is his first publication in English.

John Siberry was born Sligo and now lives and works in Dun Laoghaire. His writing has previously been published in *Poetry Ireland Review, Force 10, The Stinging Fly* and elsewhere.

Bridget Sprouls's poems and stories have appeared or are forthcoming in *Surge: New Writing from Ireland, The Quarryman*, and *The Belleville Park Pages*. In 2013 her fiction was shortlisted for the Atlantic Writing Prize.

Cathy Sweeney has previously published work in *The Stinging Fly* and *The Dublin Review*.

Esther Waters, originally from Sligo, is currently an undergraduate at NUI Galway. Having spent the past year in London, her writing is very much influenced by the city and its people. She has had work published in *Wordlegs*.

Grace Wells was our featured poet in Summer 2008. Her debut collection, *When God Has Been Called Away to Greater Things* (Dedalus Press 2010), won the Rupert and Eithne Strong Award, was shortlisted for the London Festival Fringe New Poetry Award, and has been recently translated into Italian by Kolibris Press.